CHENJERAI HOVE was born in ... He has
had a varied career, which ... e at a
secondary school, ed... and
working for a cul... CC
countries. He is curre... ...sity
of Zimbabwe.

Having been brought ... of English classics,
Hove described his first ... ...nua Achebe's *Things Fall
Apart* as 'like meeting my ... face in the mirror for the first
time'. His own writing career dates from 1981, when he was one
of the poets who contributed to the anthology *And Now the Poets
Speak*. This was followed by *Swimming in Floods of Tears* in 1983
(co-authored with Lyamba wa Kabika), *Red Hills of Home* (1985),
and his first novel in English, *Bones* (1988). *Up in Arms* and *Red
Hills of Home* received special commendation by the judges of the
Noma Award and *Bones* won the Noma Award in 1989. In
addition to his work in English, Hove has published a novel and
many poems in Shona.

He is married and has five children.

CHENJERAI HOVE

SHADOWS

HEINEMANN

Heinemann Educational
a division of Heinemann Publishers (Oxford) Ltd
Halley Court, Jordan Hill, Oxford OX2 8EJ

Heinemann: A Division of Reed Publishing (USA) Inc.
361 Hanover Street, Portsmouth, NH, 03801-3912, USA

Heinemann Educational Books (Nigeria) Ltd
PMB 5205, Ibadan
Heinemann Educational Boleswa
PO Box 10103, Village Post Office, Gaborone, Botswana

FLORENCE   PRAGUE   PARIS   MADRID
ATHENS   MELBOURNE   JOHANNESBURG
AUCKLAND   SINGAPORE   TOKYO
CHICAGO   SAO PAULO

First published by Heinemann International Literature and Textbooks in 1992

Series Editor : Adewale Maja-Pearce

British Library Cataloguing in Publication Data
A catalogue record for this book is available from the British Library.

ISBN 0 435 90591 0

Phototypeset by CentraCet, Cambridge
Printed and bound in Great Britain
by Cox & Wyman Ltd, Reading, Berkshire

93   94   95   96   10   9   8   7   6   5   4   3   2

for those killed in wars
though they never declare any
for they have no one to declare them to
being villagers wielding only spears
words, and hope.

for Johana's father
whom no one remembers
after so many deaths
so many tears
shattering many dreams
in the desolate heart.

Acknowledgements

Shadows was born many years ago when I saw two young people, lovers, opt for death instead of life. I then resolved that I would one day write their story. Now it is as I remember it, as other events have forced it to be not only their story, but the story of others as well as mine. But I take responsibility for fictionalizing it, for what it is today.

Many thanks to friends for encouraging me to write it, especially to my editor, Irene Staunton, of Baobab Books, for her encouragement and efficient editorial work. Thanks also to Laura Czerniewicz, for honest criticism and the 'shared passion for literature' which gave me the title. My thanks too, to Chirikure Chirikure, for reviving my poetic inspiration with his own poetry.

Special thanks to the Dean and his staff, Faculty of Arts, University of Zimbabwe, for the enriching attachment to the Faculty, which enabled me to write the final script of Shadows when I took up the honorary post of Writer-in-Residence at the University in 1991.

Chenjerai Hove, June 1991

Prologue

For those looking for fiction, go elsewhere, there is none here. For those looking for tall tales, find the story-tellers of the land to tell you the cock-and-bull stories. For those in search of history, go to the liars of the land. For those in search of politics, open the book of unfulfilled promises and console yourselves. This is surely no place for neither fiction nor tall tales nor lies.

I met Johana and talked to her. I swam in the river with her lover, the one in whose mouth danced a civet cat. Even his sisters can remember the life of one so strange. He was among them. He lives away from them now. Times have changed. He has changed. He will change again when he tells these tales to his own children.

Johana's father too, and his two sons, I shook their hands and saw their cracked palms, asking them how health was treating them. But to them, wars were not an interruption. Wars came and swallowed them.

They too saw neighbours die and said what have they done to die this way. They saw some of them dig their own graves before being killed. Today, no one would tell their story. It is dangerous even to mourn them.

Johanna's mother only mourned a few months ago. It was not possible for her to mourn. She does not know where they are buried. Maybe she will know some day, when the clouds of war have drifted away with the wind, away from her mind.

For now, I will tell his story, her story, Johana's story. They converged with death in their dreams of plenty and died a death which no mouth can ever describe.

This is their tale. One day they will read it, or hear rumours of it. They cannot read. They will never read. The world of written words is hidden away from them.

Johana, this girl who herds cattle like a boy, the woman whose breasts refuse to fall, she is always there, milking the cows, dehorning the small bulls and smelling of cowdung. That is the way those of us who do not go to school will end, she says. She winces her face, smiles mischievously and recalls the days of her love with the boy from the neighbouring farm, the one who drove the tractor and sang shameful songs as his head tossed this way and that, the one who sometimes drank and did not respect the elders when they told him things he did not like. She loved him, she said, because he loved her. But when he found another girl from another farm, Johana waited for him for many years. She did not hate the other girl, at least openly. When she met him with her, she greeted them both and asked about their health, the health of their families, the health of their mothers who always complained of attacks of malaria. I will go one day and see them when these cattle are tame, she would say in her heart, to them as they walked away.

She was like that for many years, going to the dip-tank, milking the cows and feeling the milk of the cows spilling down her cracked palms, warm and soothing. She stared at the little calves whose milk she took away. They will be all right, she said. I will leave some for them so that they do not die. See, they do not have teeth sharp enough to cut the grass of the grazing pastures yet, she said inside her burdened heart where many stories of love and death had stayed without coming out to dance on the lips.

Her friends said she was mad to wait for a man that long, hoping that he will change his mind. Even her own mother screamed at her once, for her foolishness. Why wait for a boy who runs around with every farm girl he comes across? Does he not see that you make the best wife in these farms where hard work and endurance are the diet of a good marriage? Does he not see that even his own mother has such respect for you? How could she not, every day you send her greetings, presents, kind words to encourage her out of her bouts of malaria.

*

The other girls sang songs to deride Johana. The woman whose head is so full of love that her eyes do not see when love is decaying. Oh, this desperate one who stores her love in the hearts of goats and sheep which she nurses like children. She will die of love, they sang, in the moonlight. Then they danced, their waists twisting, their breasts jutting out to provoke the boys in the dance arena. They insulted each other carelessly, picking on anyone they saw walking alone, someone they heard had touched the breasts of the girl who is always silent. They hurled insults at the sky, at the faces of the young and the old who indulged in love affairs which they did not approve of. No one chided them.

It was song, they said, songs must be allowed to do what they want to do. Songs are like birds, they said, they can fly anywhere in the sky. They can perch anywhere, they laughed. Did an owl not perch on the chief's head? They laughed the laughter of many years of experience with the insults and provocations of song and dance.

Then one day she waited in the forests, near the open-air church, for him to pass by so that she can exchange just a few words with him. It did not have to be him. It could be his sisters, his relatives, the ones who still hoped that the broken bricks of love would be rebuilt once more, this time into the wall of their home, the wall of a real home with children running round the yard, chickens chasing grains in the sand, brooding, waking up the neighbours with the new voices of the young roosters learning to keep the ways of the sun. She waited, not with tears in her eyes. Her tears had withdrawn from the surface of her eyes into her heart where no one saw them except her own blood, her own soul. She would suffer this for many years, silently, not a word coming out of her mouth, not a tooth showing to those who wanted to make songs out of her misery, not a crack in the side of her heart as she dwelt on the things stored inside her.

She waited with the birds too which flew across the empty sky,

11

searching for their little ones lost in the dull grass as they stretched their wings, trying to leave their mothers' nests. She saw them and thought they would wait with her. She did not want them to fly away as they always did when they saw boys wielding catapults which smelt of death. No, they will wait with me, they will sing their morning songs to me, so that my heart does not go to waste, she told her heart. Even the little grains of the brown soil clogged near her feet would also teach her to wait, she thought.

Only Sundays gave her freedom from the cows, the herds which she had to nurse like children. She waited for the man who would marry her, but for the time being, she would nurse the little goats born in the dungy sheds, the little calves born of wild cows which hunted after the juiciest blades of grass and forgot about the weak mooing of the little ones back home. She would be their reminder, telling them that young lives must be taken care of with tender hands. They too must drink the warm milk from the hard udder before they starve to death, she said, feeling the desertion of many years punishing her with its insistence.

Johana, she is here, waiting, hating her desertion as the man who drives her father's tractor refuses to come out for her. Even his relatives refuse to come near her, to console her on this day which she has taken so many years to find words for. The words of love and hatred. She would ask him, not insult her, her voice full of anguish. Did her mother not say that she should control her mouth even in extreme situations where she had no other way out save silence?

No, after all, she loved him. Her heart said so. She breathed and felt that her pulse was a pulse ripe with love. She blinked her eyes and felt the wink of love in them, in her heart, the pulse of love pouring love all over her body. This body worn out with working in the fields, harvesting maize, bitten by blades of cotton leaves, stung by the sharp edges of dry cotton bolls from which she plucked the cotton wool with such skill that many marvelled and saw how she would pluck the heart of any man out of him

12

with such abandon. She was like that all the time, and her parents said that was why she had run away from school to do the things which only hands can do. Even the white man told them that it was not necessary to send their children to school. They should allow the children the privilege of work, he said as he came to teach them how to farm the new crops which bore money like the mother of coins.

– Johana, the voice startled her at first, then frightened her when she did not see its owner. The owner of the voice remained concealed in the dense bush where the voice came from without any other movement.

Then a boy came out. He was a mere boy, Marko, the one who was learning many things from her, the one whose father did not have a farm to call his own. Marko, the boy who had to be taught how to herd cattle, the one so dark that they likened his face to the ashes of the clay pot after it had cooked a meal.

– It is you, she smiles, feeling pity for the boy who had to learn to earn money for his family so early in life. Pity, he is not a woman. Some man would marry him and help him to forget the wounds of this search for life. The children of his father would go to school which he could not attend. There was always no money, as his father said.

– Johana, if you continue saying that I am a baby with mucus on the nose, a useless boy who cannot be seen to be in love with a woman as ripe for marriage as you, I will die. Marko always pleaded. She knew it.

Then they went on to play with death, torturing themselves about what death was all about. What do you know about death, about life, to mention death and love in one mouth? What do you know about waiting, about growing up, about the little bird whose wings will never touch the belly of the sky, so many deaths, so many broken leaves which die before they can see flowers on the mother plant blooming, sucking the juices of life from the leaves, so many grains of sand washed away by river water to places where no one knew, the cotton bolls which

13

bloomed with white fluffy wool taken away to give comfort to people who did not even know what the cotton plant looked like; was that not death too? she said to him, silencing him with her power of words.

Still the boy said death was something he always saw in his heart when he saw her face. The two of them did not fear death, they agreed. They feared each other, but they hesitated in their fear of their blood telling them what they should do or what they should not do.

For many years they grew and feared themselves, the two of them, the one afraid of her age, the other afraid of her endless songs of unquenched love. They mocked at death most of the time, screaming at it in their sleep, yelling at it in their joyful donkey rides when they did not know which donkey was going to perform which tricks today.

At times they watched death from a distance when relatives and neighbours died in their sleep, or on their way to distant hospitals, or when the pregnant mother's baby refused to face the many stings of life outside. They saw it from a distance, making them feel that death was like a cloud which always remained far away in the sky, never coming near although people talked about it every day.

But they waited together for the dark things which they did not know. They sang together in the silence of their waiting. Marko waiting for his age to come so that this woman can say yes, the other waiting for the grown man who sang on the tractor, the man with a civet cat mouth, to come and say yes, rushing does not always ensure arrival, I have come for you, to take you away to the hearth of my home, my love, so that your waiting will vanish like the smoke wafted away by the wind.

They both waited for what they did not quite know, Marko and Johana. But their hearts told them it was there, waiting to be waited for, all the time. They breathed and heard their rough breath against the pulses of their hearts yearning for many things which they did not understand. Even the pulse of the rains and

14

the clouds told them to wait, even when they did not know the intensity of the rains. The rains always came anyway, they said to themselves, in the innermost centres of their hearths of desires, where desires burned them to ashes, where no one knew what was happening. It was like that too, the waiting, the tension inside them, which they did not know how to break most of the time, like the rain falling with thunder and lightning, not wanting to stop, no one knowing how to stop it. It was like that.

The seasons came and went, with the sun playing tricks on them, changing positions in the sky. Still their desires would not wane with the setting sun, or the dying season, or the dying insects which they fed on the many harsh pesticides they could not understand. They saw the sky clear itself of the rough clouds which sometimes brought thunder and lightning, killing the cattle, the goats, sometimes killing those dressed in red, sometimes punishing the earth with heavy downpours of water, the muddy water which drowned the schoolboy from the next farm. So much mourning for a mere boy, his books were not found, his clothes were in tatters, but so much mourning, so much death.

The boy with the civet cat of a mouth did not wait like Marko and Johana in the pain of silence. He sang every day the songs of these strange lands, his sorrow blowing away with the words and the music he hummed but could not hear because of the rattle of the metal of the tractor. He split the strange hard soil with the plough of the tractor, slowly laying bare the bowels of the earth, little rats scuttling away from their exposed holes, running away from the brave eagles as they circled above the boy and his machine. He turned the warm soil, breaking its roots, its veins, everything that held the hard brown soil of Gotami's lands together.

These were strange lands, the farmers said of Gotami's lands, gazing at how rich the soil was, always wondering how it was that the seeds they put in the soil did not stay there for three sunsets before coming out as little plants. It is warm soil, they said. The soil of their own ancestors had become worthless sand which gave only drops of life to their crops. It is the soil of rich manures and great ancestors. They knew it. There was nothing they could do about it. They did not even know how to thank those ancestors whose children had been forced to leave this rich earth to go to the empty lands far away from the graves of their ancestors.

This had been the land of other dreams, not the dreams of the new strangers who had bought the land from the white man. This was another land, they said, watching the warm soil twisting and turning under the power of the plough, waiting to embrace the seed which the strangers gave it. Then the strangers would thank the owners of the land, praising their ancestors in words they were not sure of. How does one say prayers to the ancestors whose praise-names one does not know? They marvelled at this soil, this land where abundant rains came and forests abounded in birds and wild animals, all singing their shrill welcome to the newcomers.

Then there was the rain which calmed down the shrill cry of the cicadas, sending the cicadas to their death in the muddy waters flowing down the dark streams and rivers of these strange lands where the morning dew wetted the shoulders of morning travellers, and rivers flooded with rich muddy water.

It was not that the boy with a civet cat mouth did not know how to wait. He did not like waiting, for anything, for anyone. His songs said it for him. Every onlooker saw it and nodded that he was created like that. Nothing would change him except death, they said, without harbouring in their hearts the wish of death on him. There were things for the eyes only, they said, the mouth should not be involved. That was the way they had come to understand the boy with the civet cat mouth, the one to whom they gave any name, one which suited the way they had woken up.

*

16

But Marko, the quiet boy who came to herd the cattle, he knew how to wait for the lone cloud to bring him a drop of rain. He waited, quiet, subdued by his intentions, his heart dying slowly inside him. He had waited before, and he was not about to give up the long walk even though he was not sure of his destination. His eyes searched for the hidden groves of Johana's face, searching for some message that would tell him he was not waiting in vain, waiting for rotten meat, as he heard the others say.

Marko sang his waiting in silence, unlike the boy with a civet cat mouth, the one they said did not have the time to lose his temper. They said he engaged bigger boys in ferocious fist fights with a smile on his face. That was his way of waiting. He waited with a shout on his lips so that everyone knew he was waiting. Marko waited in silence, hoping and yearning. He dreamt that the search would one day end with the thunder of joy, the fall of the big suspended boulder from the hill.

Johana, she too waited for many dreams which she did not know where they would end. She simply waited, refusing to die like the baby who clung to life until they say the witches of the village gathered together in the night, dancing their bewitching dances, singing their weird songs which no waking woman or man could ever understand. They sang and danced in their woven baskets in which they travelled long distances on the backs of untiring hyenas. Then a baby yielded to their calling, dying on its mother's back where she was carried so that she could share the warmth, the pain, the cold, and the doubt of blood and flesh which had matured over many years of hardships in the village. Johana, she would not die like the baby who refused to wait, the one who refused to cry the cry of meeting the earth for the first time.

One sunset, when the wars from the bush were still distant echoes from the stories of travellers, after the cows were separated from their little ones, to sleep alone so that they do not drink at will from the gourds of udders of their mothers, Marko and

Johana saw each other for the first time. He was climbing up the wooden wall of the cattle pen. She was pulling the stubborn calf which refused to obey the routine of sunset. Every day the calf had to be dragged away from its mother, to leave the udder of the cow to brew more milk without being nagged by the little one. Johana's long skirt gave away more than she usually allowed it to. It was blown away by the wind which peeps everywhere. Marko's eyes followed the wind's eyes until he peeped too, with the wind. Johana had peeped too, with the fading light of the evening sun. She saw him. He saw her. They saw each other, without words, without feeling the urge to say it. Only the discomfort of their hearts told them they had visited truly strange lands from which no survivors ever came back.

Their eyes twinkled as their hearts glowed with knowledge. They waited and searched for the words to say it, but the words refused to come. Their words refused to carry the burdens of the heart. Such things were too heavy for words. There were words which had never been found. Even the songs of the singers had never been found so that they could carry such heavy things. The singers sometimes mumbled and growled in the depth of their songs, not saying a word, but saying everything that needed to be said, everything which the voice could carry without the burden of words.

They knew they had seen themselves. They kept the silence of many years in that short time.

– Marko, she says to him, where you come from, what is the land like? She had never thought he came from somewhere, some land, some fireplace which had suckled him and shown him the world. He was simply there. She was there too, waiting together, hesitating together, doubting alone. She did not bother to see the fireplace, the breast from which he had been weaned so early in his life. Other boys of his age still stayed close to their mothers, not knowing whether they were babies or boys.

He looks at her, rather stealing a view of her face when she is not looking. He wants to tell her about the life that gave him life.

He wants to say to her, my home, that is hilly country, with caves and huge boulders standing on top of the hills. Caves which threaten you as if they would swallow you to quench their desire for human flesh. They always swallow people, these caves. Even the stories say it, about how long ago, when people and animals lived together, killing each other only when there was need for death, killing each other in tricky ways, and dying so that others might live. It was a good death. The other animals never complained. They knew the others wanted to eat, to smell blood. The caves too, walked about, swallowing people because they said it was people who caused them so many problems. The mountains had huge bellies into which they put everything which they ate with their insatiable mouths, the mouths of the mountains.

The boy wants to tell her about his mother, the one the whole village never wanted to talk to. He wants to tell her how they said his mother had things, things hidden in her pots and gourds. They said she was the one who would be killed with a nail driven into her skull.

He did not understand it, but he knew his mother did not want to talk to many people. She sang and sang all her life, on her way to the water well, on her way to fetch firewood from the forest. She sang when she pounded maize, when she ground the corn on the grinding stone, her voice mingling with the voices of the early morning birds, when birds were singing greetings to the morning sky. She sang in the morning when the sun had not yet appeared and everyone slept the last dregs of their sleep, listening to her voice as it cut through the thin night left from the dark, intense night which stood visible only in the walls of the hills where they say night escapes to when the strong sun comes with a big torch to scare it away.

But then what would Johana say, with her words, her own mouth after she had listened to all those tales. Would she say his was the house of death, the one where death had its nest, waiting all the time for the day when it would knock on the door and

19

bring floods of death? What would she say, this woman who always lived in her own silence, fearing to answer back when those with harsh words spoke?

He wanted to say all those things, but his heart felt ashamed as he looked at his toes, shy, full of shame, his face worn out with shame, his heart sunken with hesitation.

– Just like this place, with cows and calves running after each other, Marko says to her, smiling.

– It cannot be just like this place, Johana looks at him; telling him that there is something he does not want to tell her. She knows too, that if Marko ran away from home to look for a better life, he would not tell her many things about himself. Even if he told her, she too would not know what to do with those secret words. She could not go to her father to tell him that. How would her Sundays be spent if this boy went away? She did not want to go back to herding cattle on Sundays, the day she waited for the young man whom she desired for her husband, the one whose head dangled this way and that as he ploughed his father's fields with the plough of the tractor. The civet cat boy older than Marko and Johana, a young man already old enough to talk about a wife.

In her heart, she said he did not want to take her for his wife because she was herding cattle all the time, like a boy, doing all sorts of things with naughty herdboys in the forest. She felt ashamed at the thought, of herself at times when those thoughts came to her heart. Then she would not want to meet him, the civet cat 'boy' facing him in the middle of the forest where no one would explain things for her.

Johana was not good with words. They always seemed to run away from her when she needed them most. She knew she would stare at the young man she yearned for in her heart, feeling foolish like a sheep which would not cry when the sharp knife of its death was on its throat. She felt ashamed and hoped that one day she would leave the cattle and the goats alone. Yes, she did not mind helping Marko on special days, like the days when the cattle were to be driven to the dip-tank. She knew that even some mothers sometimes accompanied their sons to the dip-tank, to help them. She could do the same with Marko. But she felt the smell of the cowdung in her heart, always. The bleating of the sheep awakened her to a new day which she could not escape. She felt trapped by those smells which were so much part of her now that it was difficult to think of anything else.

Her mother said she had to do it because she must grow up. Her mother said she must leave the weak voices of the new-born calves which haunted her every time she betrayed them. Her heart told her she was one with the cattle which she herded. Johana looked at them grazing, heard the rumbling of their stomachs and listened to how they chewed the cud as they lay in the shade of the wild trees in the forest. She knew when the cows' udders were about to burst with milk. Then she would drive them home, listening to the stampede of their hooves on the dusty land of Gotami's people.

Even when she went to school, when her father allowed her to go for a short while before the fight with the teacher, the cattle, the donkeys, and the goats, they stared at her all the time, accusing her of deserting them. They stared at her as she sat among the other girls, hiding her face away from theirs, but they asked her why she was leaving them alone. Then her father changed his mind. The girls did not have to go to school for more than was enough to open their eyes to the letters of their young lovers who courted them in the forests he said. The little money there was would be spent on the boys, not the girls. Did the white man not rule it, when he said only boys would pay taxes? What was the use of sending girls to school when they did not have to pay the white man's taxes, or run a home, the father argued in the way many fathers argued when they did not want their daughters to go to school.

She also wanted to tell Marko all these things, to make him tell his own stories, but she feared his heart. He too feared her heart. And they waited for their fears to die down, to flow away

21

so that one day they could talk and sing together without fear inside them.

Many years passed in their waiting, leaving them to discern the shape of their own shadows as they grew up. Fathers married their daughters to the sons of their neighbours. Mothers waited anxiously for their daughters to make them grandmothers. If the daughters refused to make them grandmothers, at least the sons could make them so. But the little ants in the anthill did not wait. They worked hard, sweat pouring down their brows, their lips growing hardened as the anthills grew out of nothing to become huge mounds behind which the men and women, boys and girls of this new land could sit and do many things, some of them shameful, others pleasant.

Johana, Marko, they had seen each other and their hearts exploded with restrained anticipation. Days, months, years would not kill their waiting. Only the smell of cowdung, the bleating of sheep speaking to their little ones, beckoning their lost lambs, and the shushing of dying leaves, all brought their pulses together.

. . . Johana's father sees Marko all the time. Maybe he sees the long-dead shadow, but he does not doubt that Marko sits under the *musuma* tree where he sat when stories of war against the white rulers of the land were mere echoes from the voices of the lone travellers. This is a *musuma* tree which bears large fruits that grew to the size of the swollen thumb of a big man. Other boys of his age are at school, ready to go the schools of white men where only English was spoken. He sits and remembers the days when the rains fell and the crops always grew. They seem far away in youthful memory. He sits and hates his memories of the days when Johana was there and away all the time. He wonders what has become of her in her waiting, in her search for

22

her elusive lover, her hidden yearnings of the heart which she hid from all those who stood near her, those who stood far away from her, those who claimed they knew what her wrinkled face meant that day, what her quivering lips said all the time.

– Marko always sits here, says Johana's father. He sits here and says nothing. Imagine, a young man like him, refusing to leave his job. For what? Does he think he can force me to employ him when I do not want to? This land is coming to something else which our elders did not know how to name. Johana's father walks the pavements of the city of cotton, the street lamps blinding him, the cars roaring past him like ominous shadows . . .

No one knows Johana's father any more. He is alone in the city, deaf to any voices flowering around him. He is in the city, walking, sleeping, eating when he can, dreaming aloud all the time, worn out by memories. Worn out by the sting of mosquitoes which bite the flesh, the heart too. No one wants to know Johana's father any more. Johana's father does not remember any more the day he walked into the love-net set by his daughter.

– Johana, this child-like behaviour of herding cattle must stop, he says to her. This must stop if all is to go well. You are a woman, not the little girl who plays games with herdboys, he stares at her, not remembering when last he had seen his daughter so round, so calm, unperturbed by her waiting for the 'cowboy' who drove the tractor and sang shameful songs, the 'boy' with the civet cat mouth.

– What is this? he says, re-living again the day when shadows walked on their feet. I say what is this? he shouts, then runs away to the cattle-pen where Marko sits on the wooden walls counting the cattle, singing to himself, happy to smell the cowdung that has become his life. His cracked feet amuse him as he remembers the prints his soles leave on the path, with all sorts of patterns which some boys laugh at when they have nothing to do. Marko dangles his legs in the air, not seeing, not hearing anything else which is not the language of the cattle and the calves.

Marko sees the angry face of Johana's father, confronting him

23

like a bull, like a lion angry at him for playing with his little ones. He knows that he has annoyed him before, but this time he sees death on the old man's face. Marko dreams what he sees. He wakes up, then dreams it again. He fears and does not know what to say. If he says good evening, or good day, that would annoy the old man's face further. Then he sees an axe fly from the man's hands, dizzying him with its power and speed, and the fear in it carries its sound through the air. The axe dizzies the cattle, muffling their voices while they cry for their little ones stored away in their separate beds for the night. He feels the shrinking udders of the cows as the axe comes for his head, to break it, to splash his blood on the horns of the castrated bulls which he uses to draw the plough in the fields.

Later he knows the axe has missed him. He is not bleeding. He is still running, shouting only the few words which come to his mouth.

– I will die, he hears himself shouting, in the echoes of the silent forests around him. He runs away, from this home which has become his home for many years, from the man who has become his father for endless years, endless seasons, endless droughts, endless mounds of dust behind the cows grazing their way home.

Night comes, Marko does not return home. A dense night with darkness so thick that Johana's father can touch it. He looks at the fire burning outside, smoking, asking him if he does not feel the cold in the boy who has run away to die. He looks, for Johana's mother to whisper to her the deep, dark fears he felt in the last words of the boy who has become their son.

– He ran away with death in his mouth, Johana's father tells her. She weeps and brings to him the empty bottle in her hands. He takes it away from her, snatching it like a thief, then smells the woman's lips. There is no death on them. He is happy but angry. There is something he does not know. Johana comes to his heart. She has already taken the poison. He holds Johana's mother's hand as he has done many times before, at funerals.

They grieve together just as they have grieved together many times before, pain tearing them apart like a beastly animal inside them, sharing the mounds of pain, silently, without a word, even a whispered word. Neither of them knows the shape of the two bodies they will bury on the same day, young bodies tired of waiting. One devoured inside by the liquid from the bottle whose language they cannot read, the other chewed up on the throat by a hastily made rope from the bark of a tree. He would hang on the *munhondo* tree. She would lie there eaten away by the poisonous liquid until she is a hollow human barrel drained of life.

That was many years ago, when the war of the forest, the war against the white man, was rumours spoken from the mouths of travellers and strangers. Johana's father had listened to them and felt they were not very different from the story-tellers who kept the children happy every night.

But in the city where he is now no one knows Johana's father now. He left home, many years later, to sit where Marko sat, to escape the smell of cowdung which followed Marko to his death. Johana's father is alone, his heart traversed by so much pain. Maybe Johana's mother knows this pain too, but she is not here any more. Maybe Marko's mother knows this pain too, but the songs of the neighbours gave her only silence, not words.

Johana's father, they brought him home in a jeep, hands and legs manacled, and he groaning like a beast. The police jeep stopped by the road, not turning into the run-down *famu namba* 145 with its broken, decayed wooden sign-post which pointed the wrong way. The police jeep, white, pure, whined to a stop like a dog that has been humiliated by a bigger, more vicious dog.

The police constable jumped out of the jeep, received instructions in a language the onlooking children did not understand, said a few yessuhs yessuhs, and opened the back of the jeep after saluting in the dust, his thick brown boots engulfed by the thick brown earth of Gotami's lands.

The black policeman waved the little children to come over, to go and tell their parents there is police want to see them, to be quick about it because we haven't got all day in this heat that roasts people alive, heat which can kill those of us from the city. After all, it was not the police's fault that you people do not take care of your beggars and madmen. Rush about it, the policeman, black and frighteningly tall in the children's mucus-laden eyes, revealed a man from the truck, tied like the goats they have seen being sold to another farm, tied like sheep which they always see carried on bicycles or donkey-carts after the elders have talked together quietly by the cattle pen, agreeing, disagreeing, chiding each other a little, then smiling, after exchanging pieces of paper, *mari*, which everyone seems to complain about.

Money is a bad thing, Johana's father always said when he received it. Money breaks blood ties, Johana's father would smile, fingering the pieces of paper, tossing the coins into the old coat pocket patched beyond recognition.

– This farm 145? The policeman asks the mother who arrives with a baby in her arms. She looks at the police truck, wonders what crime the deserted women might have committed, feels the urge inside her to say the women were not responsible for paying dog taxes or for sending the dogs for injections at the *vetinari*. No, we cannot do that, we would not know how to answer the questions of the white *vetinari* who they say speaks through the nose as if his mouth is full of water. Even when he speaks our language, he calls people as if they are sticks or dogs, all the time speaking through the nose like one already drowning. They say he is already drowned in anger as if someone forces him to give injections to dogs instead of giving them to people.

– Hey, if your ears are sealed with maize cobs, I can clean them for you with a good slap, says the policeman as the woman walks towards the truck. Her cracked feet rouse a faint cloud of dust behind her. The baby in her arms cries, but she does not allow her to cry much longer. How can I allow her to cry in front of the messengers of the *Nkosi*, she thinks. The *Nkosi* does not want noise near his machine of fire. She brings out her tired breast, withered, drooping, and pushes the nipple into the mouth of the little one. The little one mumbles, suckles, stops crying but remains feverish as if the smell of the machine of fire were an intruder to nostrils used to cowdung and the smell of the not-so-supple breast. *Nkosi*, I was not hearing you because of the wind which blows in the other direction. This is the way the wind is in these parts. *Nkosi*. No one can change it. Every land has its own direction from which the wind blows, the woman speaks. She is near the *Nkosi*'s machine of fire, then sees the white *Nkosi* seated in the seat of the monstrous machine which she had seen ferrying away many farmers for not destroying a few cotton plants on time.

– Is this farm 145? the policeman repeats, his dull eye fixed on the broken wooden signpost, the one pointing in the wrong direction. Do you know this man? He points inside the back of the truck.

The woman comes closer, peeps into the back of the tent-covered jeep, from the back. The man groans inside. She can hear him clearly, like a beast tied to a mountain. She walks closer, like one walking to a bush where there is movement and the eye cannot see clearly what is causing the movement, maybe a snake, maybe a goat writhing with the last pains of giving birth, maybe a child bitten by a venomous snake, abandoned in the bush to die, its parents searching and searching, asking the neighbours, the playmates, passers-by, whether they have seen a lone child roaming in the bush.

She creeps closer, the policeman pushing her nearer, not afraid of touching the shoulder of a married woman. People from the city, she thinks, I am someone's wife. He touches my shoulder as if I am a small child, treating a woman like a child, a woman like me, with a baby in my hands, my own baby from my own stomach, she thinks, to herself, not telling him, the man who is the messenger of the *Nkosi* who sits inside and stares with bitterness at the dusty flowers by the roadside.

The lips of the woman twitch. They are cracked and dry. She has to lick them with her tongue, leaving a thin consolation of saliva. She holds her breast with the hand which is not holding the baby. What have my ancestors brought me to? she thinks, staring at the groaning man who wears tattered rags, greasy and torn as if the man had been picked up from the rubbish pit. She gazes at the torn man, her heart pounding inside her like the mortar she has used since she was a child, her mother reminding her to be careful, or else the grain will be on the sand soon.

Her heart, it eats her to see the man inside, in the darkness inside. The policeman jumps in, his boots cracking against the metal of the truck. He grabs the man by the leg and pulls him to the door, forcing him to turn around so that the woman can see his black face patched with wounds, the lips broken as if someone tried to slice him alive.

– Do you know him? His *situpa* says he is from this farm, the man of hard boots speaks, his tongue unashamed with the man groaning like a beast inside the back of the truck. The man he has just pulled like a bag of groundnuts, the man groaning to remind him that groundnuts and people are different things. Groundnuts do not groan, people groan.

Johana's father, what have they done to you? What have they done to the man of the mountain, the one who sneezed and the hills came down crumbling, the one whose fathers wielded the spear that bled the first of the invading Ndebele warriors, the one they sang about the whole year, women dancing their skirts away, what have they done to the mountain which breathes fire? What have they done to you? Was this your way of coming back, a man who goes away from his home without saying farewell, what thoughts are those? Then see what they have done to you. Your face, they have reduced you to a playground for dogs, the eyes are only shadows of those eyes which caught the eyes of all the girls of the land, causing them to lose sleep, weeping for you, crying that one day you would ask them to be your wives. What did they do to you . . . ? She goes on and on, the trees sending back muffled echoes to her ears, other women, other men coming to join her in the dust left behind by the police jeep as its wheels eat the road, back to the city where they say Johana's father was once seen, scrapping for left-overs in the bins, eating rotten bananas, sleeping under heaps of soaked newspapers. No one believes it, Johana's father cannot do that, a man who has his own farm, he cannot be made into a dog, they said.

But others had then kept on saying his children must go to the city to look for Johana's father. How can you let a man live like a dog? Even when his mind is dead, when his head has gone astray because of the fear planted in his heart by this war, and the fear which came to his heart when he knew that he had caused Marko's death, a man cannot be a dog, they said. They kept on saying it for many years, and others kept the flame of the old story alive. Johana's father is not dead. He is eating grass like an ox in the bush, they said. He will come back one day when he knows that 'the boys' who wanted to kill him are gone. No, how can a man's head take it all? Those from the bush come for him, calling him the sell-out whose head must be chopped with a blunt knife. We will remove all sell-outs from this land, the guerillas say. How can a man sell us out? We know, our dreamers and diviners tell us when someone has sold us out to the soldiers, they shout at the *pungwe*. Then they sing praises to his death, dancing, singing, dancing, wailing in the manner of the voices of the women when a husband is dead. They dance mock-war dances, singing the death of the coward who sells . . . but Johana's father is lucky. Someone whispers that they have already danced his funeral dances.

*

Johana's father runs away, but before he goes too far, they tell him that it is dangerous for him to be in those parts. The soldiers were looking for him all day, searching even in the granaries, searching for him so that they could make the knives on the tips of their guns drink human blood. They look everywhere, under the baskets which are piled outside by his wives. But they do not find him.

The anger of not finding Johana's father drives them mad. They take one of his sons and slice him, blood dripping from his face as they ask him, expecting answers from lips so torn apart. They call his wives and children, so they can see how a collaborator's father is dealt with, how the power of the white man is not in words, but in fight. The white man does not leave a fight half-way, the black soldier shouts. You will see that by hiding this man, you have hidden death in your basket, he threatens. He orders the other 'boys' to slice a lip, slice an ear, slice another ear, slice an eye, slice the genitals, slice the thighs, until the man collapses dead. Then he warns anyone who dares tell the white soldiers what has happened. The white man does not know how to deal with you he says. He is too kind to make you talk, the soldier goes away, his face a huge flame of anger.

The children see fear everywhere. They wish they had done what Johana did to herself long before the war came to their land. They wish they had the courage of Marko, the young boy who took life into his own hands and killed it. Oh, how strong the two were, to choose their own way of death, to do it themselves without tears on their faces, without tears in their hearts. We will die like them if we can get the strength. Only that our chests are weak. We are weak because not many people are born with strength in their hearts . . . so, quietly they began to sing their admiration for the two who died long ago. They made games on the playground in which they played hide-and-seek with death, games in which the victors were always Marko and Johana who died the same day, went to meet their different ancestors the same day, not ashamed to go to them and say we have come because we decided to come. We chose our own death. We did not want to give death the power over our own death. We decided to make death cheap like rubbish. The elders, long dead and comfortable in their death, would marvel at the two. For the first time, the two families would meet in the other world to celebrate the arrival of the two who are so young, yet so brave, young and wise ... They mocked at death, the elders would say in their old, hoarse voices.

In their small hearts, big ants busied themselves building big mounds of hatred and silent anger. They sat down after their games, watching the anger in them swell like so many boils on the buttocks of a little baby. Even the songs of the children playing in the playground, they changed. Songs to celebrate the moon hiding behind shallow clouds became songs of hate and anger. The moon is the prostitute who hides her things in a thin veil so that all can see and get tempted. The sun at sunset was the murderer who paints the sky red before going to hide in the caves of faraway places. Look at the small moon, they said, the edges are like the blade of the soldier's knife at the tip of his gun.

The mothers too, made new songs, to send the little ones to sleep. Don't cry child, the people with guns will come and eat you up. Don't cry child, your legs will be eaten one after another by those people with long knives and clothes like leaves of a thorny tree.

The new guerillas came one day, selected one of the sons of the man they were looking for. They called for his children from his three wives. We want to show you how we deal with sell-outs, those who hide sell-outs in the granary when we look for them, they said, death alive as red embers on their faces.

They gave big sticks to the sons, all of them including the small ones whose hands only knew how to make fragile wooden toys. They asked the women, wives and daughters, to sing and ululate so that a sell-out's death would not cause them any pain.

Anyone who sheds a tear would join the sell-outs. Then they asked the sons to club their brother to death, to crush his head with big sticks, to pound his brains out of his skull.

For many days none of them ate anything. They drank water and hated the taste of it . . . human blood. They all heard echoes of the deep growl of death which they had inflicted on him, watched by the owners of guns, those who threatened them all with death, what is the death of one family when we have seen whole villages killed? What is the death of one sell-out compared to the many comrades who die every day? they said, reminding the whole village that the business of selling out does not pay. Why don't they remember the man in the next farm whom the soldiers forced to dig his own grave before they shot him as he stood inside the fresh grave. The death of a lonely sell-out, they shoot and throw him away like an empty tortoise shell, they said.

All the words of their mouths reached Johana's father, where ever he was, they said. The wind carried them there, into his ears. How can a man live when all that has happened to him? His heart breaks apart, torn apart by the war fought so that we can become people in our own land. Is this how difficult it is to become people in our land which the ancestors of our ancestors left us? We wish the ancestors had not given up the fight, the fight of spears and knobkerries. A people must never allow themselves to be chained by others, they said in the heavy silence of their hearts, deep in the jerky silence of believing and unbelieving, the silence of doubt and burdensome stories which do not have the courage to leave the lips.

Johana's father roamed, lost in the memories of the stories they brought him. No letters. No pictures. Nothing. Only stories of a home finished by death, the home where only ashes are left, the home of mourning, the home of rivers of blood, the home rejected by its own ancestors. What has a man done to have his ancestors turn their eyes away from him like this? they wondered.

The man went to the city where they said the soldiers obeyed some laws. There were too many people watching them so that they did not kill anyone they came across. So they watched the people of the city, hoping that one day they would travel far away from the shiny city, to the roofs of their homes where they were born. Then they will be shown what the earth carries for them. They will be shown that the gun is the weapon of power and humiliation, not a thing that simply dangles from the shoulders of strong men in green uniforms that makes them look like leaves in a city full of glass and white paint. They will come home one day, the soldiers told themselves as they watched the women writhing their bottoms around provocatively, but at the same time refusing to sleep with soldiers whose roughness everyone said they knew. They watched the men in smart jackets and ties, behind small desks in the corner of *Nkosi*'s office, pushing neat pens, signing what they did not know. They watched them and said to themselves: The son-in-law will see the mother-in-law's buttocks on the day they have to cross a flooded river together.

For many nights and days, Johana's father slept in the big house at the railway station, the big house where many people he did not know came, waited for a day or two, took a train and went away to their own lands of their own problems. He slept, sometimes, but he was woken up by the policemen wearing thick boots. They wanted to see everyone's papers, *situpas*, train tickets, all night. Johana's father learnt the trick of those who stayed for many nights in the big house, those who did not have relatives in the city of cotton. Buy a ticket, they said, then you can go every day and say you have changed your dates of travelling. He tried it, with his face looking like an angel, honest and clean. The man who sells tickets was sorry for him, sorry for the death in the family, and gave him another ticket.

But one day, the policemen who do not wear uniforms found out the trick. The sleepers heard the heavy thudding and plodding of boots, the whole police camp descended on the big house where people waited for trains. Everybody was woken up by the harsh voice of the leader of the men. He gave short orders and they saluted him before running away to do whatever they were told. Everyone was asked to take your things and follow. Anyone who runs away will wish they had never had feet stuck below their bellies, the Sajeni ordered.

The policemen packed the men and women in a small jeep, took them away without explanation. At the police camp, many dizzying questions were asked until no one remembered where they came from, or what their names were. Questions, questions, questions until Johana's father said yes to all of them. Are you a fool, yes. Are you mad, yes. Are you a thief, yes. Are you a terrorist, yes. Are you a rapist, yes; until he dozed with tiredness, until the Sajeni kicked his mouth, splashing blood on the floor, ageing teeth scattering all over the floor like grains of sand on a windy day.

In his head, his wives sang songs like children dancing for joy when the first drops of rain wet their faces, licking them like the tongues of the little puppies. They sang insulting songs about a man who runs away from his home, a man who does not want to fight a snake which has entered his homestead, a man who holds his wife so that the intruder can rape her properly, a man without shame. They sang on as he lay there, bleeding, hearing the faint questions of the policeman flooding his foggy memory of things.

Many days later, he woke up in a new place which he did not know. There were others too, some lying on the dirty floors, some eating their clothes, others making games of the urine as it spouted from their things. Everything was the way no one has ever told him things could be. Groans, blood, laughter, smoke of burning rubbish, dung heaps, vegetables torn apart as if they had been grown in the play-garden by children.

They kept him like all of them, throwing food at them, sometimes splashing cold water on to their naked bodies, making

34

them shine with drops of water. The bodies glimmered in the cold, the men and women growling and cursing at Petronella, the girl who kept them, mentioning her mother's private parts, cursing at the womb which harboured such a monster with no heart inside her.

But the keepers of the place shouted back at them all the time. Even when they stood nearby, asking them for their names, they shouted. No, Petronella said, you cannot be called Johana's father. You must have a name, she laughed the explosive laughter of women at the well. Petronella was satisfied that the things that happen to the head cannot be known. So she laughed. Ah, this one, calling himself Johana's father, the other one saying he has no name, the woman next door screaming that she will not sleep if she does not have a man this night. Whatever happens to the heads of human beings to make them into such beasts, Petronella wondered in her mind.

– I mean your name, the name on your *situpa*, you hear? Petronella laughs at Johana's father. He gazes at her as if the whole world has left him, leaving him gazing at something more frightening than a red sky. In his heart he feels the pain of Marko, the boy who died many years ago before the guns came to his farm. He feels the pain of Johana, his girl, the one who was so close to the smell of cowdung. They died together, happy to help each other in death. He knew that strangers or friends must not be invited to death. Although one may not invite a visitor to come help me die, they had invited each other, he thinks inside his head.

– I am Johana's father, he says gently, the voice sinking into the depth of thoughts, things which are never said. Write that, or do not write anything. I am not a cow that you should write down my name, my owner, everything as if I do not have a home. Write that I am Johana's father, that is all. I close my mouth and seal it, the man carries out his threat, sealing his mouth with dry, cracked fingers.

Petronella stares at him and sees many things which she has

35

seen in the faces that always come to the place where they keep those whose heads carry snakes and stinging black ants. Sometime ago, they had brought a girl like this, always refusing to tell her name. A man came looking for her, trying to awaken in her the love she had for him when they were small children in school. The girl looked at him and spat in his face. Love was rotten, she said. For how many years does he think love will remain green? A mango survives one season, ripens, falls away and dies. No mango ever remains green for seasons, she told him. Go away and marry your own mother. The man went away, sad, tears streaming in his eyes, looking at her chained like an animal. For many years he came to gaze at her through the fence, mourning her, pleading with her to be his wife, tearing his heart apart. They took him to those who know how to look inside closed heads. Those who know how to look inside heads said his head was not correct. He went to fight the war when he was too young to see human blood.

All those things which he saw in the bush, they are coming back to him now. They took him away to I-don't-know-where. Maybe they will chain him up some day. Maybe they will keep him all the time until he is an old man. No one knows. Petronella remembers, traversing the whole map of pain she has seen from the time she left the school where they teach young women to take care of heads which are not correct. Petronella remembers the many words, useless words which streamed from the many mouths of those whose heads were not correct. Useless words of things which are muddled up, memories muddled up with many other memories, death mingled with life, blood mingled with breath, useless words of tomorrow and yesterday mingled together like many different grains of sand.

Petronella, they say, your job is a dangerous one. One day you will end up like that too, her relatives warn her. If it is the money, you are a pretty girl, find a job as a secretary or something. Then they give up on her. They say madness is like white paint, you can smear it on to those who sit next to you.

They seal their mouths and say no one should say we did not say it.

When Johana's father asked them to set him free, they said he was not in jail. So he need not worry about that. When Johana's father said he was not mad, they said that was why he was there.

As he argued with them, some of the keepers of the place thought his words were sensible. They gave him a leaking tin and asked him to water the garden. He tried once and told them the tin was leaking. They stared at each other and nodded in mischievous agreement. Their eyes shone with discovery, like naked children the moment they discover they are boys or girls. They each went away to write in their books, each agreeing with the other. Johana's father should be freed. He surprised us one day by telling us that the leaking tin he was using to water the garden was leaking. What an exciting moment to us all. Hence we highly recommend that he be freed forthwith . . . and they mailed the papers and told Johana's father that he will be free when the papers come back. They did not listen to him when he asked them why they sent them away in the first place. If they are the same papers going to come back, why did you have to send them away? he said. I want to know. You yourselves, with your own mouths, told me that I was going to be free because you are satisfied with me. So where are the papers going? Johana's father wanted to know.

At sunrise one day, they let Johana's father out. They wave their hands at him. Inside himself he says he is not a bus or a car to be waved at when he passes. Town children, they have no manners, he curses. He walks away, barefoot as he came. There is no dust to mark his path. There is no blade of grass to prick and tickle the soles of his feet. There are no sticks lying around to entangle his legs. Even the creepers which he hated so much when he went hunting on his farm, they are not here either. Only the tall, straight trees line up the pavements like buildings.

He walks alone, not knowing where he would like to be. He walks all the time, looking ahead at the sky far away, hearing the threatening voices of cars and people passing by. He is not alone because the voices of his wives sing to him about the father who ran away from death, the man who let his children inherit his own death, Johana's father. Johana's father who threw an axe at the boy whose father no one knew until the boy went to hang himself by the tree next to our homestead. Johana's father, the man who sowed death in his fields. Oh, what does a man who sows death harvest? Those who sow seeds harvest maize, those who sow death harvest what? But Johana's father, why did you marry us when you had death in your pocket? Johana's father. Johana's father. Johana's father.

Many voices of children, of women, of boys and girls in the playground. He hears them as he walks along, drained of all that he had lived for since he left the home of his ancestors in Gutu to go in search of better lands to farm. It was the fault of my father, he says. Every day he opened his mouth, yelling: children, your buttocks have nothing to bring you, only the foot has something new. The wealth of a man is in his hands, he said, all the time.

After many years of those painful words from his father's heart, Johana's father heard that the white man was kind to those who worked hard. The white man, *Nkosi*, was happy to give them farms which they could own if they worked hard. They could become buyers of land. No one would rule them in their own land. Even the District Commissioner will not have power over you. You will be the masters of your own lands, obeying only the laws which the white farmers obey. The lands which we want to sell to you are infested with tsetse flies, but they will be a thing of the past. The white man has power to kill all of them in a short time. Do not think the power of the white man is only with guns and jails, he has powerful herbs too which can kill tsetse flies in one day, they preached to the men.

Johana's father was persuaded. He asked his eldest son . . . to come with me so that I can see the owners of those lands which

38

they want to sell to us. How do you like the idea of me getting rid of the headman who insists that when I kill my own goat, the liver is his? I know I have to leave the land which swallowed my ancestors, but they know that a bird which does not fly away to search for worms will never get fat. Johana's father tells his *dangwe*, the first-born son who would inherit everything which the father would leave when the time came for him to lie by the anthill, as he always says with his own mouth. You don't want to inherit poverty, whispers the father to his son.

The son gazes at the distant sky, bare, and the hill of Gutu ablaze with intense heat, the soil bare and desolate. He has heard of the street fights in the city of Gweru. Blacks are fighting blacks, and the jails are full. He fears the thought of standing in front of the white man. He has heard many stories of the white man not being able to say which face is which, especially black faces. What will he do if the white man says he was the one seen killing other blacks far away in the city? One never knew with the white man. It saddens him, but his father is persistent like the heat when the rains refuse to come.

His eyes rest on his father. The son nods, thinking about going to faraway places where his father would be buried alone, at some lonely piece of land where no other man from the blood of his ancestors was buried. He would lie there alone, with no one to share the anthill with, no one to say to him, this is our place for many years, let us remain here and give our children the confidence of our death. They will follow us too. The son hears his dead father's song reminding him that he wanted to lie in the same piece of earth with his ancestors, lying together with my own blood, he hears his father say . . .

Take me and bury me
in the lands of my ancestors,
not in this bare land
where there is no umbilical cord
from the blood of our birth,

take me and bury me
at the home of my ancestors,
under the soil which bears our name,

the son hears the familiar song which the elders sing in the dark of the night at every beer party.

But for now he would accept his father's decision, he would come with him to the District Commissioner to accept that he was prepared to go with his father and never run away to search for jobs in the city. If you run away to the city, the police will run after you, arrest you and lock you up in a house with high walls so that you won't see the sun for many years, the interpreter speaks, revealing the hidden words of the young white man. He imagines how it was possible that a man could be kept in such a house for so long without going to meet his woman, to talk to his father and learn the ways of going ahead with the blood that he borrowed from his ancestors. How can that be, a man in a fence for so many years that when he comes out his children would not remember him? How can that be? he said to himself, hoping that the interpreter was not adding little nephews to the stories coming out of the District Commissioner's mouth.

The old man waited silently, not knowing what the District Commissioner was writing on many pieces of paper which came from large boxes, from small boxes, from dusty boxes which came from other more dusty boxes. The tools of the white man, says the old man inside himself. He saw the way the white man's tea appeared without anybody saying tea should come, the way the white man drank the tea after taking off his glasses, reading silently from one of the papers, putting on the glasses, removing them again so that he can clean them with a white piece of cloth. He saw it all, the way the white man, young enough to be his child, stared at him as if Johana's father had come to tell him about his problems.

Then the white man carefully took his pencil from where it was planted, waiting to vomit many words which Johana's father could not decipher. He was blind to the words which lay there on the pieces of paper, but it did not worry him. What is the purpose of sending children to school if not to increase one's eyes, he says to himself. The white man, he knew his ways, he thought, not like our children who refuse to learn even the way to make scotch carts. He felt some anger welling in him as the white man continued as if the two of them were not even there.

He remembers those who said they wanted to chase the white man away so that they can inherit all his things. Joshua Nkomo, he says to himself, do you think you can take the ways of the white man and do better than this young man who was born with it in his blood? Listen to the way they speak through the nose? Even when they speak our language, we cannot hear them, he says to himself, to his heart. His eyes see it all and marvel at the way the white man does not even seem to think about what he was doing.

The man's heart pounded when the white man started stamping on all the papers, writing quickly on them in a way which no one can ever read. Then he gave the papers to Johana's father, warned him about behaving himself well when he goes to his new farm.

– The papers say all the good things about you, says the interpreter, don't go and shit on the laws of the country when you have your own farm. The white man has been kind to give you a good recommendation so that the Land Board does not refuse you the permission to buy the *Nkosi*'s land, the interpreter speaks, his voice high like one shouting to people the other side of the river. When you get there, go and see the District Commissioner there. He will know that you are a good boy, paying your taxes all the time, doing everything as you are told. That way you can sit under the same shade with the white man, the voice sinks slowly into Johana's father, making him feel like a child who is going to school for the first time, a child who must not do this or that without asking for the teacher's word, a child who must work hard so that he can learn the ways of the white man, a child who must listen . . .

... and when he walks out of the place where the white man works, he steps on the floor carefully, feeling sorry for stepping on the white man's floor. It is only the interpreter who shouts that he must teach his son to follow his ways, to know that *Nkosi* is *Nkosi*, that was the way God created it and it must remain like that until trees come out of the soil roots up with leaves in the soil.

Johana's father is happy that he can tell Johana's mother that he will soon own his own piece of land where the white man only comes after Johana's father says so. A piece of land where the only people sleeping in the mud huts are people who know that this land belongs to Johana's father. Imagine, Johana's father will be like his own chief, his own everything. The only time he will go to the white man is to sell his crops so that Johana can go to school to learn how to read secret words from the man who will marry her. Johana, she will learn many things on the farm, and she will tell everybody that her father is soon going to be a *matenganyika*, the buyer of land, the owner of his own piece of land.

Johana's father knows that the headman will be far away in his memory. His piece of land, where he can plough the amount of land as his heart wishes, it is where his children will not be beaten for allowing cattle to stray into their neighbour's badly planted fields. Oh, mother of Johana, imagine, planting vast stretches of land with rapoko so that we can brew as much beer for our ancestors as we want. No one will come to tell us to grow this or that. The headman will not be there to speak the words of the District Commissioner, demanding taxes and a goat for the small things which he thinks he does for us. We will be on our own, asking our ancestors to keep us, not through the headman or the chief, but with our own mouths. Mother of Johana, things might be hard at the beginning, but they say the white man is clearing the land, removing all the wild animals that are still found there. He will use big guns like those which killed Hikira, the man whose spear was silenced by the spear of the white man.

Lions are like ants to those big guns. We will be happy, bringing our children up the way we want them to be, not the way the headman wants them to be. They will be our own, we will be their own, he sings it in his heart, happy that the tears of his face have been wiped by a kind hand, happy that no ant can now nibble at his toes.

He is a master farmer, he remembers. Do people not remember how the white man who teaches the good ways of farming came to our house, spoke a lot of things many of which no one could understand? Did he not mention my name so many times that people thought I was the younger brother of the white man? Every time he opened his mouth, his tongue danced with my name on it. Who in the whole village has had the white man come to praise him in his own home? They were jealous, their eyes looking at me as I stood there next to the white man like his interpreter, nodding as if I could understand the language of the nose.

Johana's father, he dreams like this for many months, for many years too. When the letters come to tell him that his farm was ready, waiting for him to go there, he refuses to go. How can they say there are flies which eat cattle there? What sort of flies are those? The white man must not be trusted in these things. This is why the white man does not want to learn our language so that we can speak face to face. Maybe that interpreter was told all those things and he decided to keep them in his heart. People have bad hearts, I tell you. How can they tell me that I cannot take my cattle there? What is a man without cattle? I cannot go around boasting about owning donkeys and goats. Even a woman does not do that, the man mourns his dying dreams.

Many months pass, Johana's father knows he has fallen into a trap. How can a home not have a bull for the ancestors? Flies that eat cattle, who has ever heard of a thing like that? This is the way to trick us, he cries for many days. He does not sleep any more.

A few days later, he takes a bus to this faraway place to see for himself. The Land Board says all the farmers must come and see which farms they want. But they must know that they have to be careful. It is land which no one lives in, full of lions and elephants, mosquitoes that can cause serious illness. Johana's father carries the letter with him on the bus. His son comes with him, wondering where this land of big flies is, wondering whether he will see real lions or small animals which someone could not find a name for, and so called them lions to please them.

Johana's father, how he will miss the familiar birds eating familiar grains. How he will miss the stumps, the rocks that impregnate the landscape. The memory of his eyes will fade from the scenery of birds following unfamiliar paths of this empty sky. His children will bring him nestlings whose names he does not know. He gazes at the fruit tree which coughs to him the remains of its inside, for the children, to rouse their youngish appetites. Johana's father, his name will fade from the memories which have given it refuge from dream to dream. He walks and sees the sky for the last time, formulating new versions of exile to a land whose rivers flow upstream. A man weaned from the leaves, from the blades of grass whose dust he knows so well. He will not be here for many more years. He will not be here for many more months. Exile wields the hammer of dark memories. Where the victim and the victimizer embrace, who shall intervene, and clouds of rain pour down on the sky's rejects.

Johana's father walks in the wide plain, seeing, feeling the scars of his departure. He does not know what the sun will say, tomorrow's sun. He looks at the sky, at the hills, at the little rivers which grew up on his laps like children, then the smells of flowers that will one day ripen when he is not there. The lonely bird, the ominous secretary bird, paces pace after pace, counting the remains of insects which scramble and scamper. The chop

44

chop chop of the familiar beak irritates him with its threat of absence.

From tomorrow, from the day after tomorrow, from he-doesn't-know-when, he sings inside himself, the ominous bird will sit on the rooftops of his huts, announcing the evil remnant in the old homestead. There are many homesteads which will remain intact, with children and dogs chasing after hopeless bones and fireflies. But his home will not be a home. It will be a home of graves, ancestors, shadows, broken walls leaning on tired earth.

They know him well, Johana's father, in the village of his birth. He sings work songs at the beer parties, he mediates when young lovers decide to shed the skins of unmarried passion. He is there always, singing, dancing, talking, working, telling the stories he has told before. But tomorrow's sunset will not see him here. He will be a visitor, going, coming, arriving, departing, greeting, shaking hands, not singing the familiar songs which are part of his tongue.

– Johana's mother, you must get ready soon. It takes time to get ready, to move the whole home to another place, the man says, his mind away, not knowing how it feels to be exiled in a land whose graves one does not know how to describe.

– We have already asked Tapiwa's mother and the other women to help us, she answers him.

Good woman, his heart says. Good woman.

– I hope our friends will not think they threw some bad words at us to make us leave this place, he hesitates.

– No, they know the poverty of this soil, answers the woman.

– Yes, but we are not the only ones seeing the poverty of the soil, Johana's mother interrupts him.

– Johana's father, another man's problems cannot make me lose my appetite, she laughs. Don't they know that different people do different things when faced with the same problem? She says.

– Yes, good food is nicer eaten with your neighbours, Johana's father adds.

They talk on and on, about what they will do with the huge pots which Johana's mother used for brewing beer. What about the chickens, those sitting on the eggs all the time? And the little calves which no one can allow on the train? What about the schoolchildren? Are there schools where we are going? Children should learn to read. A blind person is as good as dead these days. On and on and on and on, their hearts full of this new feeling of things they do not know.

Johana's father looks at her, then at his feet, determination welling up in him.

– When the small bull grows horns, it must learn to defend itself, the words flow out of his mouth on their own.

– And to leave the graves of our ancestors because we feel like small bulls with small horns, she protests with soft words of the heart. Can we be small bulls even in the eyes of our ancestors? The words pain him. This woman, she says bitter words, sweet words, with the same mouth. How can she cut the soft places of the body with such a blunt razor? Leave her alone, his heart tells him. Leave her alone for the time being. There will be time for such painful words, words which kill a man's desire even for alcohol.

Johana's mother, she will not know the name of the stone from which her grinding stone will be made. She will not know the name of the wild fruit which her children will bring home. She will stare at plants which resemble the wild vegetable, *rude* which she cooks every day. She will not know whether to pluck it and take it home for Johana's father's meal or not.

Johana's mother, she will not know where to have her metal pots repaired when their buttocks wear out and allow the water to seep through into the fire. Ah, the path to the well, she will also not know the way to the water well, the path to the river.

Kwedu kune nyimo
Hakuna mandere
Kune nyimo

Hakuna mandere

Kwedu kune nyimo
Hakuna mandere
Kune nyimo

Johana's father watches the children go round and round and round, singing the names of familiar food, familiar rivers, naming familiar trees. They name them all, telling each other how the rivers give one another water.

Mukuvi flows into Ngezi
Ngezi flows into Runde
Runde flows into Save
Save takes all the water
to the land of the endless waters.

The children all sit to the rhythm of song and handclaps. The one left standing, trapped by ignorance, starts all over again, tracing the drop of water from rivulet to stream, from stream to river, from river to endless lands of water. The children name the fruit trees, the animals, they name them all and play games. Then come the love songs. How they jump and recite the old songs which gave many marriages to the land of the ancestors.

Sarura wako kadeyadeya wendoro chena
Sarura wako kadeyadeya wendoro chena.

Wangu mutema kadeyadeya wendoro chena
Wangu mutete kadeyadeya wendoro chena . . .

But that day when Johana touched his naked body, with its tiny puddles of water spread on the glistening dark skin, her fingers did not feel that this

47

was death. It was life, dark life from which she felt she did not want to be redeemed. She lay there on the white sand, her body withered with the power of this new discovery. She had discovered a body which she had carried for so long without knowing its power, its weakness which was like a lizard's tail, its uselessness in the form of this other power which forced it to endure so much pain without yielding to the voice which always told her to run away, to hide behind the rocks, to drown in the water with shame. Johana, she says to herself, this is shameful, but it is also good feeling like this. It is the way to feel when you are alone with this man, this young boy who should be a little brother. This is the way to live, not to die, she says to her silent body, to her subdued heart.

Johana then knows that this sunset will always be different from other sunsets her dark eyes have seen before. The songs of the birds will be different from now on. The birds will sing the songs of what happened in the shadows of the smooth river rocks, of what will always happen. The woman's silent lips tell her the words refuse to come out of her. They remain stuck in her mouth, under the tongue where they say wells of saliva sometimes drown words before they come out of the mouth.

Many years passed in her body, as if the time she had lived a different life had been wasted, thrown away like a leaf blown away by the whirlwind . . .

Johana's mother remembers, faintly, many years later after Johana had taken her own life in the faraway lands of Gotami.

They sing, all the children learning to describe the looks of the one they want to marry. They describe the breasts of the one who should suckle their child. The one with the long neck is mine. The one with breasts bursting with milk is mine. Boys, do not take the one with a gap in her front teeth, she is mine. Girls, the boy who plays the banjo is mine. Can't you see the way his eyes devour me as he plays the banjo?

The children sing about every familiar thing, *nhengure*, the bird, chasing after owl for cheating the other birds for many years, threatening everyone with horns which were not there.

The herdboys too, sang their songs and danced them in the forest, speaking to the monkeys and the baboons, insulting them, ridiculing them so that they would not come to steal from the fields. They sang and shouted to see who received the loudest echoes from the frightening caves where leopards and snakes knew each other's kingdom.

Familiar songs, familiar birds, familiar faces which everyone sang about, thought Johana's father. What will the children do, what will they know? Who will tell them about the things which we have in our hearts, the rivers in which we washed and sang the songs of sunset? Who will tell the children how the white man took away the land, this land, that land beyond the hills, how the white man envied it and told us that if we have no money to pay taxes, he will take away the land, he will take away the land in which their fathers are buried. Who will tell the children all these stories?

Uncle Chaita was good with those stories, the one who remembers even the songs of the birds on the day the white man brought bulldozers and police came with harsh words in their hearts and on their mouths, cursing and destroying even the waterpots of the women in the huts. Chaita, he tells the children these stories so that they know. He is like a child that one, always with the children, making them laugh all the time, telling them the ways of the white man in Joni where he worked on the mines until his toes were crushed by the big machines in the mines and they could not keep him there any more. He knows our ways and the ways of the white man, so he teaches the children so that they can know the ways of the world.

Johana's father walked back home, his heart refusing to unburden itself. He was hurt inside like one who had a big fire burning inside him. He burned inside until the ashes were so dense no one could clean them. The hearth inside the heart has no one to remove the ashes. Talking is the medicine for troubles, he tells himself. A silent man will die in the silence of his foolishness.

Johana's father turns to continue on the path to the beer party. They will shake hands with him. They will ask him how his wife is. They will ask him how his children are playing. Some will ask him how his home is. Johana's father will say they have life, the home is safe. He will say he came because a man who broods about his problems alone is likely to bewitch others. Talking is the medicine for troubles.

Johana's father, this land where you are going, they tell us it has flies so big they can eat a whole cow and finish it. Are those words of itching mouths or they are true words? They say there are so many wild animals that even a big man like myself will ask other strong men to accompany me to the bush to help myself? Are those words from bad mouths or what? Tell us. The only way to quench thirst is to go to the well. Tell us.

They ask him endless questions about the fruits of the new place, the hills. Are there lions or leopards in the hills? Does anyone know the name of the fruit which is abundant there? Tell us, Johana's father, you could not fail to ask people from there when you went to see the farm. How about the rivers? Some say the rivers of that place flow the wrong way, up hills and slopes. Johana's father, don't let us listen to rumours when you can tell us all these things. And the sun, they say it comes from the wrong direction like the rivers.

After a few quaffs of the home-brewed beer, Johana's father begins to tell many stories of how he saw the footprints of a lion. Some man in their group shat in his pants, cursing his ancestors for throwing him away like the empty tortoise shell. What have I done to be thrown away like worthless seeds when the juice has been sucked? If this is what my foot can carry me to, I choose the buttocks which make me sit near the grave of my ancestors. The lizard with a broken tail must learn to play near the cave.

– It is great land, the land whose rivers smell only of fish, he says.

– The land of many rivers which puzzle you with the way they flow, but do not listen to the tales of the beer party, he remembers saying to the old man who would not imagine how this son of the village would be a stranger in other lands.

– There are fruits too, but we will be taught the names of those fruits. The *sumha* of the place are big like the fist of a young boy, he goes on, into the night.

– You sleep on your mat, lions and hyenas cry in the forest, waking you up, but none of them comes to attack you unless you have offended the ancestors of the land, he tells them.

– The problem is the mosquitoes, big ones as large as the finger of a man, he winces his face.

Marko's mother remembers . . .

That day Marko walked home on the cracked path, knowing that the earth had said to him what it had never said before. The words of the birds, the cruel songs of the animals which yielded to the urges of the setting sun, they hurt him gently inside him. They tickled many things inside him. Marko's head was full of so many confusing things. He listened to the shrieky voices of the insects, sometimes wishing he were one of them, sometimes wishing he could be the little bird which the mother bird kept under its wings. He did not know what to do with his body which had sent so much fire into his life. All he knew was that the day does not come where another was. Things change, he said to himself, his eyes shying away from looking at the body of the woman he had touched. This is the woman with whom I have defiled the land of Gotami. She always told me that the land of Gotami was holy land which must not be defiled. But the urge of the body had made her kill the vows which she had not made herself. She had found them there. He also had found them there with the power of the ancestors of this strange land of shrines and rituals. He had walked naked on the soil whose ancestors, and their children, he did not know. It was this land which many people feared in a way which he did not understand. Many stories said wars that had been fought with the Ndebele warriors had made the land holier. The people of Gotami had shown all strangers that their land was the land in which the bodies of their ancestors lay, only to come out of the soil with strong voices which even the deaf could hear. It was like that, he thought. This land is the land of the ancestors . . .

Marko, my child, death is not a stranger in our home. You are the child of death, born when death was looking through the window. swearing at the umbilical cord which they took away to bury in the soil of your ancestors. The way to die is not the way to live.

This child who was born with all sorts of things on his face. A friend of diseases. Why did diseases attack you in the wrong places all the time? Why did they not leave you alone? A boil on the buttocks, a swollen tongue, a knee that refused to bend for many days, teeth that grow one on top of the other. A head that sweated and sweated until you were dizzy, with all of us waiting for something to happen. You refused to die on my breast, the breast of sour milk.

Then people said all the things which their mouths could say. She is the mother-witch who wants to eat the flesh of her own little one. The woman is in trouble. For many years she has been eating the flesh of other women's babies. Now the time has come. They have asked her to bring hers to the fire so that they can eat hers also. The woman is in big trouble. She does not want to have the flesh of her own child eaten. When they bewitched him, she unbewitches him. That is why the boy is nearly dying all the time, they went on saying all these bitter words far away from me so that they could reach me through the mouths of those who always say I heard from someone who heard from someone who heard from someone else. Then how does one go and ask someone who heard from someone who heard from someone else. See, there is no one to ask. There is no mouth to tell the story.

A child cannot stand the words of elders. They kept telling you when you were growing up, they said words about the way some people are born unlucky, coming from bad wombs. I know that they told you these things so that they could hurt you, killing you with words before you even knew how sharp words could be.

Words can be sharp, cutting the heart where no one can see. Then you groan in the silence of your sleep. You walk the paths of the village like a cripple, your heart broken to pieces. That is the way words can take the place of spears. Have you not heard how the chief spends all his time trying cases of how words came out of someone's mouth and pierced a heart, making it lonely for a long time? The chief says it is the mouth which ends up eating big logs. The tongue is the small fire which ends up eating up big logs. Words are like that. They cut deeper than razor blades. Razor blades are better. They cut where you can see. But words are not like that, they cut where you cannot see.

Your mother has things which she keeps in a gourd. Listen to them running around in the night. You must leave her before it is too late. Otherwise you will eat had-I-known. Don't you know that had-I-known should never be allowed to come after the event? Run away to other lands where you will grow up to become a man who can marry a wife. If you want to die leaving some footprints, run away and leave this death alone.

They poisoned your heart so that you could run away, leaving the breast which fed you, the hands which held you. You abandoned the back which carried you. How can you do that to a woman who was alone? Even your father could not drink his beer in peace. They sang my insults at beer parties. They sang insults at work parties, telling the whole village how evil this woman with cracked lips is. Look how red gourds spoil the beer. A beautiful woman, if she is not a witch, she is bone lazy. Listen to the words which come out of the mouth of a beautiful woman. They are poison which causes sleepless nights, they sang for all the village to hear so that they could refuse to fetch water from the same well as me.

Imagine, the whole village refusing to fetch water from the same well as me. Can a child like you stand that? Can you stand up with strength and say my mother is my mother no matter what words you have to say? It is hard like stone, but this is worse.

Death, you ran away from death, to another death where no one was there to tell your ancestors how to handle a young death. An old death is better. Everyone dies when the years have left them behind. Everyone joins the womb of the earth on their way to the ancestors. To die the way you died, that is pain. That is pain which eats into the heart of a human being like the rat which eats the cracked feet of a sleeper. The sleeper tries to wake up, the rat blows some fresh air on to the wound so that the sleeper can sleep until the whole sole of the foot is a big wound.

Marko, this child born to die far away looking for another life. They say it is hard to run away from your own nest where you were born. Now you are back. Now they bring you back. You went away on your own feet, walking. Now they bring you back on their feet. You walked away and they carried you back. That is the death which the people who went before us chose for you. Nothing you could do. When the earth speaks, even the deaf hear. They listen carefully because things of the earth cannot be allowed to leave without entering the ears of all.

Did they say the woman you shared death with had a baby in her womb? Tell me, was that your baby? Oh, how the two of you refused me a child of my own child. How could you share death like that? Did nobody tell you that a stranger is invited to a feast, not to a death? How did you invite a stranger to die together? Imagine standing by the village path, saying to a passer-by, come over, please do not go away faster than you appeared. The stranger will avoid all the paths which pass through that village. He will sing songs of how he was one day invited to die, not to live. He will dance it in the arena and everyone will look at him as he points in the direction of the village where people are invited to die. They too will dance with him. They will remember the village of death. They will sing songs about how the people of the village of death plant death even in their fields. Death in the fields, the season of harvesting death.

Johana, they say she had a child in her womb, a stranger who was invited to this earth from other lands where those yet to be born live with their friends, waiting, talking, refusing invitations and accepting others.

Stranger in the womb, why did you accept to enter the fire of so many deaths? To say yes to a journey which you know will end up in the house of death in such a short time? It is painful. Wounds are always painful even when only the scars remain. They remain painful. The pain goes inside and hides there. That is why people always say of this wound: Oh how Chatora's dog almost killed me; this wound, how I fell from that rock behind the big tree with sharp thorns. Wounds never heal. Only we pretend that they heal. They remain there to say, my name is the gate of death. Death wanted to enter through this small gate, but the ancestors told death to wait.

Johana's mother will always have in her mind the day . . .

. . . they took Johana's father away, he was ready to be a wounded corpse. He died in my eyes, here, standing here in front of me. He died. He knew that he would die that way. So many other deaths had told him that he would die like that. He walked away a corpse, dead. He walked away with feet which did not feel any pain, dead feet.

Johana's father. He told me he should have died a long time ago. I am like a ghost, he said. He remembers the stories which went from mouth to mouth, saying they had got him, saying if the soldiers did not get him, the fighters from the bush got him. So many stories that you could hang them on the leaves of all the trees of the forest.

That was the way he always said it. I slapped him one day, with my own hands. He was angry with me, but he could not hit me back. He had vowed in his life that he could not slap me because I was his *vahosi*, the woman who would kneel with him at the shrine of his ancestors to ask for health and friendship in the family, the woman who held the hands of many families together and made them share blood, the same blood. I slapped him when he said death was always looking at him through the window. He felt death in his breath.

Johana's father was not afraid of death. He said a man who runs away from death will run into death. He laughed about it, drank his beer and slept peacefully. Sometimes he saw Marko sitting under the fruit trees, waiting for some fruit to fall. Sometimes he saw his two sons, running away from him. He never spoke about seeing Johana, the girl who carried the name of his mother into the grave. She has her grandmother's name too. They brewed a lot of beer for the ceremony to give her the name. People danced the whole night, singing their voices hoarse. They sang and danced until they forgot about tiredness. Some remembered tiredness many days after the dance. They were happy. So happy they put away pain for a while so that it would not disturb them.

For many years I sat with Johana's father, telling stories of how we would grow crops, sowing seeds, harvesting well so that our children would not starve. We would send them to school so that they can know the ways of the life of the city and the white man. Who does not want to have a teacher for a child? We said they would become teachers, standing there in front of the children, telling them how the world worked.

Johana did not do well in school. She cried all the time the teacher told her to do the things he wanted her to do. When she played, the teacher beat her until she refused to go to school. Johana's father went to fight with the teacher but it made things worse. He only wanted Johana to know the secrets of words written in the letters from the boys seeking to share life with her, bearing children with her. He did not want her to become a teacher. She would be hard-headed, he thought all the time, like the daughters of the businessmen who always went out with any man they wanted, refusing to listen to the advice of their parents.

The head teacher then swore never to see Johana's feet walking in the school yard. She will die ignorant, the teacher said. She

56

will die ignorant, stupid, with the head of a goat sitting on her neck. Wait until you see the way the world is going. She will not know her way to the well, the teacher shouted at Johana's father. They say all the children in the school laughed until saliva poured out of their mouths.

My Johana will stay at home. This school is not a war where children come home crying every day, Johana's father said. He put her on the bicycle carrier and rode home. Did the white man not say that we had our own piece of earth where no one can insult us? Did he not say even the teacher was paid from money which we pay to the council? How can a man who works for another man begin to behave as if he is the one who gave a job to the one who gave him a job? If a man overeats and then takes a spear to stab the granary which stores the food, he should not blame someone else when tomorrow his stomach starts rumbling with hunger.

We grew crops in the fields. Sometimes the rains came, sometimes the rains did not come. But the children always had enough to eat. They did not walk around with bare backs. The children missed those familiar songs and faces which they grew up seeing when they were young. They sang new songs of their yearning for the old hills which were part of their hearts. They started searching for new names for the trees and rivers of the new place far away from the land where they grew up. It was painful. I saw it on Johana's face, the pain of not knowing that this pain comes from this part or that part of the body. The pain of those who bleed to death without knowing that they had a deep wound. That can happen in the months when it is cold. A cut does not pain until the blood is warm enough to feel the pain. The children were like that. They were in pain, much pain without knowing it. We saw it, but we said, the wounds will heal. The children will sing new songs talking about their life here. They will sing about the waters flowing in the rivers of this place. They will hear the new echoes of their voices from the new caves of the hills of these parts.

It took many years for the children to stop singing the songs of yearning for their old friends, the old rivers in which they bathed knowing that nothing could disturb them. Here, only those who knew the laws of the land went to the rivers to wash. The laws of the land had to be learnt. We then knew the land did not belong to the white man. There were people who owned this land many years before the white man came. They came to teach us the laws of their ancestors.

Every land has its own laws. The rivers, the hills, the trees, the animals, they have laws which must be obeyed. The white man could not teach us those things. He did not know the laws of the rivers. He did not know which hills were holy and which hills were not holy. He did not know which animals were to be killed and which ones were not to be killed. They say the white man does not know that to live well in a land not of your ancestors, you have to brew beer and ask the owners of the land to ask their ancestors to welcome you . . .

But Marko had a deep joy in himself, the joy of defying the words of the ancestors. He had conquered Gotami's words and remained walking with bare feet on the land, watching the dust from the hooves of the cattle, smelling the smell of cowdung from the shining bodies of the cattle. Even the smell of the fresh milk mixed with cowdung from the cows told him that his heart had been torn apart by this woman who now walked silently to her parents. She would be silent for many years about the story of the river. She would not have the courage to tell it. Her parents would never know, he felt inside himself. She would not stand there in front of her father, telling him the floods of joy which flowed in him, in her, the glistening body splashed with drops of water, the mangled hair sprinkled with sand. How could she tell the story which only the boy and the woman knew? And the pain too, she could not stand there and tell them the story of the blood which burst out of her, of him, the droplets of blood seeping into the sand she looked on without wiping it away with her finger or her worn-out dress. No. She would not tell them. She would face the anger of the ancestors of the land alone with him. He would face the anger of the land alone, with her . . .

This was the land of Gotami, the big chief who led his people in the fight against the strong fighters from the lands far away in the west. The Ndebele fighters, they were all over the land, plundering, killing, taking away the beautiful women, the young men to be made warriors, the grain. Gotami was here, leading his people who lived along the big river, Sanyati. Gotami's people knew how to ask their ancestors for fish from the water. They fished without fearing the sharp teeth of the crocodile. They knew the herbs which made the crocodiles sleep while the men fished and the women fetched the water for the children.

They say when the Ndebele came, they asked to see Gotami himself. He told them they should walk in the direction they had come from. He cannot talk with people who come to his lands armed with spears. His people hated human blood. The only blood they saw was the blood of the wild animals which they trapped or speared to death. The Ndebele impis must walk back before many things happen to them, Gotami said.

The eyes of the Ndebele impis itched for the blood of the young men of Gotami's land. They went from hill to hill searching for granaries. They searched for cattle to kill so that they could roast the meat and eat. How can strong warriors fight their enemies on empty stomachs? They searched in the hills, in the mountains, everywhere. But they could not find Gotami and his people. They were angry.

A messenger came to them again pleading with them to go back to the land of their own fathers. Gotami must not be angered by people roaming his land, not knowing the laws of the land. Gotami will not have that.

The impis thrust many spears through the heart of the bearer of the message. They did not know that in Gotami's lands, the bearer of messages is not the bearer of scars. He is only the carrier of a message. If it is a painful message, the anger should go to the one who gave him the message. They killed Gotami's messenger because he had refused to tell them where Gotami's caves where. When he died, the only words he said were something whose meaning the impis did not understand. *Gotami mupare*, he shouted as he fell, his body torn with pain.

It is said when the impis started their search again, they found many pots full of groundnuts, steaming hot. Their leader went nearer, calling on his warriors to come too. He was amazed. There was no fire to make the pots steam like that. He whispered to the senior warriors about this strange behaviour of Gotami's people. His eyes had not seen anything like it.

But the young warriors were already shouting, pleading with their leader to let them eat the groundnuts to show Gotami that his herbs are nothing in the face of the might of the Ndebele warriors.

– *Akudliwanga lokhu, kuyahlola madoda*, the chief of the warriors said. This cannot be eaten, it is a bad omen, he went on, pleading with his fighters.

The warriors would not hear it. No army could stop them. They wanted to destroy the insolent Gotami after eating his witchcraft. *Ngumthakathi*, they shouted. He is a witch, he must be killed. He is a witch, he must die for it, they said.

Their chief persuaded them, but no ears could hear him. In the end he said they could eat, but ears which refused to hear might not continue hearing for many more years.

The warriors broke the pots in the scramble to take the bigger ones. They ate the potfuls of groundnuts. Many shouted as they ate, with mouthfuls of groundnuts: *Kumnandi kakhulu*. It was better than any groundnut dish they had ever tasted.

They ate and ate, but they would not finish. Their bellies swelled until none of them could walk. They continued to eat as if they could eat for many years to come. Many slept as they chewed Gotami's groundnuts.

The story of the death of the Ndebele impis at the hands of

Gotami's groundnuts spread for many years to come. Johana's father heard it from the elders of Gotami's people.

They came to the land of the *matenganyika* to tell us that the land did not belong to the strangers. They could farm the land, but they must not work the fields on Thursdays. That is Gotami's day of ceremonies and rituals of the land. And they must not work the fields on Saturday mornings, that is the day when Gotami's *mhondoro* appeared and roamed the land in broad daylight.

Laws of the land, Johana's father said, they must be obeyed. The children learnt all the laws for children also. They should not insult any animals. They should leave the baboons alone because the baboons of these parts will not steal from anyone's fields, the elders taught the children.

When some strangers refused to obey the laws of Gotami's land, strange things happened to them, their children or their fields. Those who were strong church people were the ones who said the only laws they knew were the laws of the great God of Joseph and Mary. But many things happened to them.

But Johana's father said Gotami's laws have to be obeyed. Nobody has ever told him that Gotami's laws are against the laws of the god of Joseph and Mary.

Pain comes and goes. We made new relatives, new uncles with the same totems as the other uncles we had left behind in the land of our ancestors. The homes were far apart, so that no one accused anyone of witchcraft. We worked hard, our hands cracking with work. We saw the children grow and felt our hearts settling down. This was our home, we said to ourselves. Johana's father began to boast about the way his itching feet took us so far away, to these lands where we worked hard until we could buy machines of fire which we had only seen far away in the farms of the white man.

War came. We wished we had not followed the itching feet of

Johana's father. But it was useless. Many people talked about how many more people were dying in Gutu where we had come from. Every day someone dies there, they said. Even the radio which Johana's father bought for us, always said it every night. So we sat and sighed. When death has come, no river can stop it from arriving.

For many years, Johana's father would farm the land with all his heart. Sometimes the land rewarded them, sometimes it remained stubborn, conniving with the sky to punish them with dry seasons, failing them in their dreams of this land of plenty. But they always knew in their hearts that the soil in these parts was better than the worthless sands of their homes which they had escaped. It was better here, they said. After all, they were not as far away from the graves of their ancestors as the relatives who had gone far away to North Rhodesia, they said to themselves.

The soil was sandy, but still warm from the many years of its virginity. No one farmed it for many years. The leaves of the trees fell on the soil, to be swallowed by the insatiable throat of the earth, manuring the land. So it was sandy, but still warm enough to rouse the inner urges of the seeds which Johana's father and his wives put in the soil with hope.

The tall grass too, it grew and then dried up, only to be swallowed by the soil where it had come from.

The women and the men felt the warmth of the soil in the cracked soles of their feet, in their palms as they weeded the fields. The soil stuck to their feet and palms, like brown patches on their skins. They did not mind. It was life.

Johana's father breathed warm air and felt it was the gift of this new land. He felt the warmth of the soil in his heart. The soil too felt his presence in its new heartbeat of ploughs and planting, harvesting and ploughing.

There were hard days too. The mosquitoes gave them malaria,

biting them in their sleep until they woke up dazed by either illness or the longing for their familiar paths back where they came from. The few cattle they had been allowed to bring in this tsetse fly area soon died, leaving deep scars in their hearts. They learned to mourn when an ox died. They had never done it before, but it came out of their need for the companionship of the animals. Many small things changed without them seeing.

Then the men from the white man's offices came to teach them how to grow different crops. They should not waste their time growing maize. They should not waste their time growing rapoko and other crops which their parents had taught them to grow long before they were born. No, they should grow cotton so that their children could get money to go to school. Cotton was the king of cash, they said, teaching the farmers the manner of preparing the land, the manner of planting the seed, the manner of tending the frail plants so that they could flower. Salesmen came to sell them bottles of poisonous liquids. Cotton must be sprayed with these poisons if the farmers were to harvest something to sell to the machines of the white man far away in the city.

It was not easy for Johana's father. How can a man say the crops which the ancestors left him should not be grown on the farms? Even then, none of the farmers had learnt how to grow this crop when they worked hard to obtain their master-farmer certificates. They had grown maize and rapoko, the crops of their ancestors. These were the crops which gave food to the children. These were crops which they would put in the granaries and sit in the shade with pride because the children were not starved for food.

They could not understand how a man with a family could grow crops which the children would not eat.

When the farmers wanted to put the white man's fertilizer into the soil, Gotami's people were not pleased. They were sad and angry. They would not live to see the soil of their ancestors defiled with the white man's medicines. They would perform rituals to tell their ancestors how the strangers wanted to defile the holy soil of their ancestors. They would come to the hills of their ancestors and speak harsh words so that the farms of the strangers would fail.

Johana's father touched the soil with the fingers of his hands, smiling sometimes, sad at other times when the rains did not come, sad at times when too much rain came and washed away young fields, fresh with the seeds in them. The man still continued to dream of better days ahead, seeing hope in the pregnant clouds which hung over the fields. He knew then the soil was his only hope. So he sought to speak with it, to understand this soil in whose belly the people of Gotami would not allow them to put fertilizers.

The people of Gotami refused to allow Johana's father to spray poisonous liquids in the fields. It was a way to destroy the soil of their ancestors. Those little insects were the insects of the land of their fathers. They should not be killed by careless hands. They should be allowed to fly free with the winds. The ancestors would be angry with them if they poisoned both the air and soil, Gotami's people warned.

Johana's father said it was all right with him. For two years he farmed the land without poisoning the soil with the white man's manure. He did not defile the air with the poisons which some said were for making the strangers impotent. The white man is clever, they said. He does not want us to increase our numbers too much. So he thought of the poisons which would make the farmers infertile for the rest of their lives.

– Johana's mother, what worries me is what the teachers of farming say to us, Johana's father intimated to his wife.

– Are they not the ones who went to school to know the good things to teach us? she pointed out to him. She remembers how he once forced her to listen to the young man who came to tell them to abandon the crops of their ancestors. That was long ago when they were still in Gutu, learning to be master farmers.

– Mother of the child, it is good to grow the crops of the white man. But to leave our own crops out is not good. It is senseless. When you learn the good ways of other people, it does not mean you must leave your own good ways. Imagine, our children will not know the crops which our fathers taught us to grow. The man wore a more serious face, his heart troubled by so many thoughts. He did not know what to do even as he saw the burdens which the white man's farming gave him. First, it was in conflict with the ways of the people of Gotami. This was their land and no one could remove them from it. Then, what would he tell his own ancestors after abandoning the crops of their blood, the crops through which he would be able to speak with them?

Yes, the people of Gotami had been moved further west, to the country of dry rivers. They moved to lands in which nothing grew. They had fought with the white man, sending elders to the seat of power of the white man. But the white man would not change his mind. He was the one whose ancestors had arrived many years before, wearing long trousers, and the elders had called them 'the ones without knees'. In those years the elders thought the white man could not bend his knees. But now they knew he could not bend his thoughts once they started moving in one direction.

The elders would not hear that strangers from all parts were coming to plant their crops on the graves of their ancestors. What will Gotami say? They protested in bitterness. How do we know whether the strangers will respect the holy shrines of our ancestors? The people of Gotami were bitter, chewing their hearts in deep turmoil. But the white man, young though he was, said he could not listen to them any more. He sent surveyors to mark out farms, warning that if any of Gotami's people greeted the surveyors, the next visitors are going to be armed with real guns.

This was the land where Gotami's people lived for many years. Now they were no longer there. But their hearts remained in their land, refusing anyone who wanted to defile it with the white man's medicines. The walked through forests and mountains to

65

return to honour the shrines of their ancestors. Do not plough here, they said, this is the grave of my ancestor, the one who hunted lions and leopards. Do not build your houses facing this direction, our enemies once came from there. They taught the strangers to be careful with many things. Their hearts and souls remained in the land of their great ancestor, Gotami.

Now they were here again, reminding the strangers that the crops of the white man would kill the souls of the ancestors. Johana's father knew the meaning of their words. How would they brew ancestral beer if they were not allowed to grow the crops of their ancestors? How would they honour them with bulls when the land was full of flies that killed cattle? How would they marry younger wives when they did not have cattle for the bridewealth?

The troubled mind of Johana's father swelled in him every day. He wanted to talk to his wife about all these things. She listened all the time, but she could not do anything. Sometimes she would gently blame him for allowing himself to be cheated by the white man. Why, he did not tell us many things which he is now telling us, she protested. She too felt the pain of this exile, of being in the land to which she did not belong. She did not know the rules of the land. Even if she knew them, she was bound to confuse them and make mistakes. Nobody could learn all the ways of Gotami's land in such a short time. Mistakes would happen, and Gotami would be angry. She did not want to die a bad death.

The day she met the boy who sang on the tractor, Johana had taken her father's four oxen to the dip-tank, to kill the ticks which drank blood from their bodies. The white man had allowed them four oxen, nothing more. It was like that for all of them, all the new farmers in these strange lands. Her father always felt she was unsafe to go alone, with her little sister, Tariro, the tall and weak one whom they thought would die of malaria one day.

Mucus always flowed abundantly from her nostrils, like a weak spring from which endless streams always gently flow. Johana did not mind. She argued that four oxen did not need several adults to come with them to the dip-tank. In Tariro, she had someone to share words with. That was all she wanted.

It was far away, but there were others who came from further, like the boy whose father already owned a tractor. He was far away, beyond the hills, near the river of big fish with teeth. The people of Gotami always passed through Johana's father's home, eating some food, or drinking a few gourds of beer before they plodded on to the river where the father of the boy who sang on the tractor made the boy work so hard, uprooting trees, chopping them, sometimes dragging them with huge chains behind the tractor, then chopping them to bits. He would pile them and wait for a few weeks, or even months, before setting them alight, huge flames that went up to the size of hills and forests, a forest of fire, they said. The boy set them alight in the evening when it was getting dark and cool. It was hot country, and he did not like to feel the streams of sweat pouring out of him. It was better when it was cooler. He could go into the forest of fire without feeling so much pain from the heat.

But on the day when cattle had to be dipped in the dip-tank, he left everything and drove the four oxen they had to the dip-tank. He sang as he drove them, instructing the young boys who came with him to keep their eyes on the oxen. He sang Ndebele songs and sometimes danced to those songs which not many people understood, without bothering who listened. They should sing their own songs if my Ndebele songs annoyed them, he said, with his usual laughter which cut across the empty fields. He did not care about the mounds of dust from the feet of the oxen. He did not care about his feet as they got dirty and dusty. After all, they said his tongue was dustier than anybody's in the whole area.

Johana saw him bullying everyone at the dip-tank, shouting and cursing if anyone let his ox mingle with his father's four huge oxen. He said everything which came to his lips, challenging them to an immediate fist fight. Some dared come near, making sure he might see their size and swallow his words. But the boy who sang on the tractor would take off his shirt, his black muscles showing clearly like straps on his body. His long hair would not budge. Then the tall giants would warn him about his mouth in which a dead lizard laid its eggs, a mouth in which a civet cat lives. They would tell him that death is not something to be afraid of where they came from. But the boy would look at them, challenging them to leave tongues alone so that the people could see what a fight was all about. If you do not know how to fight, why do you talk? he would rumble, his whip already on the dusty ground, eyes darting here and there so that no one would attack him from where he could see.

– If I knock you down, I will urinate into your face and you will never utter a word, the boy laughed. They said he was mad and left him alone. Punching someone and then urinating on the dying face was the last shame anyone wanted to go through in front of all the strangers. So they left him alone. They looked at each other, their eyes talking secretly, and then spat on the ground. We cannot tell, they said, the boy's family must be haunted by evil spirits. Then they left him alone, cursing inside their hearts, cursing at the strange land which makes them see all sorts of things which the eye should not see while it is alive. Cursing at the new land of Gotami for letting their ears hear all these stories from the young mouth of the little mad man whose tongue had no good word stuck to it. But they left him alone.

They left him alone and learnt to laugh at his insults. He would insult them with the private parts of their fathers or mothers, but they would simply laugh and forget. Things from his mouth were to be laughed at, they said, otherwise you kill the boy and his evil spirits come into your head, they consoled themselves.

Johana saw it all in her quiet way, her mouth sealed, her heart intrigued by this boy who sang on the tractor, the boy whose mouth opened and fire came out. She saw him and his bare feet, treading carelessly everywhere. She knew the type of person he would be when he became old. The reckless old man who says whatever comes to his mouth, the father who did not care where his children are, the man who went to the beer drink and came back after many days, chasing after the pleasures of women and drink. He was like that, to change him would need many days of hard work and talk.

She saw him for many days and nights in her heart, sometimes asking the weak and tall Tariro to say her mind. Tariro was too weak to have a mind, Johana thought. She always said those things were not for people of her age. Why not ask mother if she knew what to say. Only big people had answers to such questions, Tariro would say, taunted by words from her sister.

Sometimes parents talked about the children of the neighbours, how they were brought up, how different lands bring up children in different ways, how it was not easy to find children who were like their own, coming from different lands. This is the land of strangers, they said. We have met from all the directions of the earth, how can we be the same? This is our problem. They yearned for the days when they would know the ways of the children of their neighbours, the days when they brought up children together because they cared for them, they were children of the village. This was different. Children belonged far away to the lands of their own fathers where they were brought up in different ways.

The boy who sang on the tractor was always talked about. Some said he was careless and spoiled by the mother who always brought him food in the fields as if she were his wife. They have sisters, why do they not bring him food? they said.

Even Johana's father sometimes took interest in the words of his children when they talked about the children they were trying to play with. Some people are like that, he said. But I hear he works the farm day and night. At night the tractor chews the soil, pulling the big plough behind it, he confessed his admiration for the boy who sang on the tractor.

For Johana, the words of her father did something which she could not understand. They ate into her heart, causing her sleepless nights, nagging her in all her work. She even named the little calf 'cowboy' because they always called him that way. Nobody knew his name yet. They said whatever name they gave him, the boy did not mind. He wanted so much to laugh with everybody that he had no time to argue them out of their foolishness. If he was not laughing he was looking desperately for a fight. Johana knew it and it bothered her. How can the boy be so full of so many things at the same time? Inside her, a voice of fear of him always called to her, as if it were her saviour from far away places. She wanted to see what would happen with this boy whom nobody knew how to handle.

On the day they met face to face, she had gone to the river with her sisters to bathe in the wide waters of the river of many fishes. She had not bathed in the river for a long time. She missed it. She missed the sight of her own body in the open, lying on the round-bellied rocks after swimming in the fresh water of the river which smelt of all kinds of fish and plants. She had done it with her friends before they came to this strange land where children were warned not to stray too far from adults because the spirits of the people of Gotami did not want stray children defiling the holy hills and rivers. The wild animals also roamed all over the place, wetting their mouths with saliva, waiting for the boys and girls to visit the bush so that they could eat the soft bones of the children.

Johana missed the cool feeling of plunging into the streaming waters, without care and worry. This is the way she had grown up in the lands of her own fathers far away. She missed it. It was not a big thing, but she felt something had escaped her life. She wanted to swim there in the open river, to feel that some

70

tormented eyes were stealing in on her body, to run and search for her clothes after the wind had taken them away. She wanted to be alone with her body, not caring about clothes and people. Only the eyes of the wind and the trees were the friends she wanted to share her body with, nothing else.

At the river, she took away her clothes without looking first to see if any eyes were feasting on the young breasts which sprouted on her chest. She took the clothes off, plunged into the cool water flowing so slowly that she did not feel the weight of the water pushing on her body. Her body felt the water in her armpits, nibbling coolly at her like a rat without teeth. Then she splashed some water on to her face, getting wilder and wilder as the other girls shouted at her. She felt their excitement too, in the water splashing on her face, on her body, on her dark shiny skin.

Then the boy with a civet cat mouth appeared from behind a rock. He stood there and watched her bathe. He did not speak although she knew he wanted to say something, to ask her to dress up while he and his friends searched for another place to bathe. He stood there, no words coming out of his mouth.

– It is good to wash in the cool river water, isn't it? He spoke at last, turning to go away like one who has not seen anything.

Only when he had gone did she think that he had seen her. She had not felt that before when his face confronted hers, when his eyes looked at her and saw the breasts which threatened him like the gentle horns of a young calf. She knew the smaller girls were shouting at her to stop bathing because a man was coming! But the sound of the water, the excitement which she felt in her blood, made her deaf to everything, blind to all the things she was supposed to look out for when she bathed at the river. But for now, she smelt the smell of the fish and the decaying leaves piled at the edge of the river where the water did not move. She smelt the smell of the mixture of the smell of her own body with the sandy water which smelt of fish.

Her heart settled with the comfort of the river water and the sound of the water as it plop-plopped its way among the rocks.

Dark rocks felt like people watching her, dumb, deaf, unmoving. She felt in her heart that she was sharing the secrets of her body with children, these rocks which did not know the deep things of the bodies of adults, of girls like her as they grew up from the sleep of childhood, knowing how to hide their bodies and how to take care of them. She saw the water flow past, with little leaves and feathers floating, on their endless journey to the land of endless waters.

Then Tariro stood there, talking about the way the boy who sang on the tractor looked at her, as if searching for something which he had lost. She laughed the laughter of little girls who are beginning to discover that bodies should be hidden most of the time, except in sleep when one accepted nakedness as something which no one could cure.

Tariro, this mad girl whose head was full of laughter, she said she would tell her mother that the tractor boy saw her sister bathe without her sister running away to fetch her clothes. She said it was a thing to laugh at to see a woman run away to fetch her clothes when men shouted if there was anybody bathing at the river bend. How do you know that they ask before they have feasted their eyes for a long time on the body of a woman? she asked. Men can do such things, they are funny, she told her sister as they walked on the dusty path home.

For many days, the sun beat the earth and the water gave more pleasure in its coolness. Johana felt the bath was like a saviour to her. She would go again with the other girls from the other farms, the girls who bathed in their own ways of jumping and kicking at the water. Even the tractor boy's sisters, being strangers to this land too, would come also, watch her in the bliss of her river bath. They would befriend her and ask her what the rivers are like where she came from. They would ask her if she wanted to be married to these strange lands or go back to the land whose people she had grown up knowing their ways. They teased her all the time, telling her that her own fool was better than any other fool since she would know the extent of his foolishness before it went too far.

Johana did not know most of the things. She said her father was here, why should she leave him to go back where they came from? What would they do if her father fell ill or wanted to perform some rituals where they had to be present? What would they do if her baby was ill and the only person who could cure her was her mother who was so far away in the land of Gotami? She did not know all the things she wanted to do. She did not know, she said, shrugging her shoulders, baffled by the many questions they asked her and wanted her to answer.

They told her they would go home, home to the lands which they understood, the lands whose fruits they knew how to name, the lands which were full of people, not these lands which overflowed with wild animals and insects waiting to kill everyone they saw. No, these were not lands for new brides like them, they said in their mocking ways. And they sang the songs of their faraway lands, twisting their waists in the *agogo* dances and *jikinya* dances of their faraway places which they missed. It made their longing grow more and more all the time, the desire to play on familiar rocks and swim in the pools that had brought them up.

Then the girls taught themselves to play. They took the mud from the river, painted their bellies and danced the dances of the river, the dances of the old women whom they saw dancing leaning on their walking sticks. They sang about the boys of this place with their placid sexual behaviour.

The boys of this land,
Where are they
So we can see them?
Come out and see,
Come out and see us
The girls with giraffe necks.

73

The girls of this land
For how long can you hide?
Come, see the girls who walk like guinea-fowls
Come out and see, the writhing waists.

They sang and danced till the sun theatened to abandon them to the animals and the insects. Johana felt she would not reach home before dark. She feared her father's anger and the anger of the animals which roamed the bush and the sky. The vultures and the lions, she thought, they told each other where the next kill was to be. Then they converged to tear away the dead flesh of the animals, happy to eat and leave some for others roaming in the forests.

For many days, Johana did not know how to persuade the urge inside her so that she could be the same again. Before, she had felt alone, without any strong inner urges compelling her to fly with the little birds which disappeared into the clouds. But now, she looked at herself and heard the voice of the boy who sang on the tractor. She heard his voice soar into the sky, mingled with the rippling of the river water as it found its way through the rocks.

Johana sometimes admired her naked body soaked in the water. But at times she hated it, thinking it made her swim clumsily, or feeling her body caused the other girls to say some bad things about her when she was under the water. All the time she was alone, with a deep inner urge to be somewhere, with someone who would tell her from the bottom of his heart that her body was now the body of a woman who could bear children with him.

She sang to herself, her lips moving, not moving, her chest heaving with the sound of an unheard song deep inside her. She sang songs whose meaning she did not know, songs which made her cry without knowing what it was she was crying for. These were songs which sometimes hurt her, but also gave her a small dream to keep to herself so that nobody knew.

– You have changed since you started going to the river with

74

the other girls, her mother shocked her one day, the sun piercing the girl's eyes like a needle. It was a Sunday, the day she would be free to go to the river after milking the cows. She knew the cattle would not see much of her on the Sunday. After the church service under the *mupani* tree, she did not have to come home with the other girls who lived beyond her father's farm. They could come alone, leaving her to go with the sisters of the boy with the civet cat in his mouth. She knew it as her mother hopelessly looked at her, waiting for an answer which the young girl did not have.

Her blood had told her many years ago that she was now a woman, not a girl to be scolded over everything. She was a woman now. Other girls of her age already ran their own hearths, cooking for husbands and children.

– I don't know the meaning of your words, she said, her finger scratching the top of her head. These itches seem to come at queer times, when things were hard and there was nobody to rescue her, she thought. Usually Uncle Chikwepa, the one whose mouth was already on the side because of the pipe which was always in his mouth, he would rescue her, asking the mother not to make his little mother miserable with difficult questions. He would laugh and say something about a day never following another day's footsteps. Things must change. Even the sun changes. The little bird which perched in one place all day soon fell off from the tree, dead, he would say, smiling with his teeth heavy with the soot from the tobacco. Johana's mother would notice how Johana was feeling secure in the wings of a protective uncle, the one who knew that little eggs must not be crushed with a big stone.

Johana looked at her mother and wondered. She did not know what the mother meant, or the words she would use to answer her. Her words swam into the heart of the girl like a little fish which nibbled at the tiny leaves floating in the river water. She felt them but did not know how to remove them, the little fish nibbling at her own soles under the water, tickling her inside

75

with the things she did not understand. There is no defence against words, they would say to her. When a word has entered the ear, it spreads its mat there, they said to her all the time. Now she was seeing it with her own eyes. You have changed, the words of her mother rang in her ears like the school bell which many people said told the children they were late and the teacher was angry. You have changed, the other girls said, and she heard their words inside her. The pain of not knowing came with the echoes of the words to her inside ears. There were many things she did not know. She knew it and felt that was the only thing she knew well.

Johana told her mother not to worry herself. She was happy with her friends with whom she could play at the river. She told her how they joked with her, telling her that she will be their brother's wife, the one who sings on the tractor. They poked fun at her, how they were going to have to sing songs of marriage to praise her, insult her, doubting her womanhood. For their brother, they would sing praises, but add a few insults on how his head got so lost that he could go away into the bush to hunt, only to come back with a kudu which had died of some sickness. The sisters of the boy sang to her, showing it on the river bed how they would dance the insults to the new wife. Their feet made patterns on the sand, a little dust shooting up in the air, wafting along like some perfume from the little flowers on the river bank. She saw it all and laughed the laughter of joy and doubt.

Then one day they brought her a letter written in a dull pencil. They persuaded her to take it, but she refused. If it was not a letter for her father she would not take it. She did not know how to read. Why would anybody write her a letter? Who was that who did not have a mouth to speak the words which he put on the piece of paper? she asked them. She did not want to offend her father. She had always been told that she must bring any letter straight to her father, she told them.

The sisters of the singing boy were confused. They tried to be gentle with her. They called her the one with a giraffe neck, the one who walked in the rhythm of women planting groundnuts. But she simply smiled and called it the clever tricks of the python which entertained its victims with bright colours before capturing them. So it went on until the boy with the civet cat tongue decided to meet her himself, to say it with his own mouth.

It took many months before she said yes to him. She said yes on a hot afternoon. He had waited for her until she finished bathing in the river with the other girls. His sisters arranged everything. He walked home, through the dust and the grass, taunting her, getting annoyed, annoying her, wanting to give up, but somehow her eyes telling him that she would succumb to the weight of love. His heart waited for the moment when her knees of love would collapse. Then she would be his, searching for him in all the bushes, annoying other girls with words about him. He felt it and kept on.

Some day she would say yes, changing the strange land to something else which both of them would not know how to handle. They were strangers in this land, strangers to each other, strangers to themselves, meeting strange dreams of this land which they say Gotami did not want the strangers to defile.

But in the burning heat of the afternoon, she said yes and gazed at him, her dark eyes dancing with passion. Their eyes met and narrated many stories to their hearts. He did not know what to do next. She did not know what to do either. They were now in the land of confused passions, not knowing which step to take like people stuck in the mud of love.

– I will marry you when the times comes, he said, holding her hand, feeling the humility in her blood, the yearning and the silence of many years. She did not speak to add any more fire to the fire of his words. She took them and stored them in the inside of her chest, hidden away from anyone who would want to steal them.

– I am late at home, she said as she disentangled her fingers from this man who would marry her, the man who sang on a

77

tractor, the one with a civet cat mouth. She felt in her heart that her father must not, from that day, be called Johana's father.

That day she walked home, hating to hear her mother call her husband Johana's father, hating to hear the mouths of her friends call her mother Johana's mother. She felt she was Johana, waiting once more for the words she had heard to be repeated in her ears so that her heart would swell with pride and dreams. Soon she would be called so-and-so's mother herself, she said to herself, with deep contentment. She would be so-and-so's mother too, like her own mother.

For many days and nights, she dreamt in her sleep, she dreamt in her work. She was alone in her dreams, inviting the boy who sang on the tractor to dream with her, wondering if his mother would dream with her, not knowing if her dreams were mere dreams, empty words from the mouth of a madman.

Many sunsets would pass before the boy came back to her with new words. Many nights would ache in her body before she knew what he would do. Many mouths would say many words about them before she would hear him repeat the words which she yearned to hear.

Then came this boy she taught how to herd the cattle, how to walk the soil of the farm to which she was no longer a stranger. She showed him the fruit trees of the forest, the little rivers from which the cattle and the goats would drink to quench the thirst which haunted them in the sweltering heat of the land which had been changed after only a few years. She would also teach him the ways of the land, how Gotami's people wanted their land to be respected by all strangers so that they do not offend the ancestors in their graves.

Gotami's people do not allow you to shout at the animals, even the baboons in the hills. Do not insult them, she taught him, showing him the footsteps she had taken so many years to walk, sometimes with pain, sometimes with itchy prickles. If you hear the honey-bird singing its song, be polite, kneel down and thank the people of Gotami first before you follow it. Watch the way it flies. If it takes long strides from tree to tree, it means there is danger where you are going. It will say things in a sad way, warning you that it is throwing you into the mouth of death.

Have they not told you the story of how a stubborn man followed the bird without thanking Gotami? Oh, the man was led into the mouth of death. He was led to the nest of pythons, the one where all pythons live. One python swallowed him. Inside the python he found all Gotami's people assembled, old men and women, sitting at the *dare* to try him for all the laws of the land he knew he had despised.

– Did Gotami's children not tell you about Gotami's holy days? asked an elder. The man could not answer. They had warned him about his foolish ways but he would not listen. They warned him, they sent his own friends to bring him the word of the gentle anger of the people of Gotami. But the man remained deaf, deaf to any warnings which stopped him from his ways.

This is my farm, the man had said. This is the only soil I own, bought with the money of my own sweat, he said. Go away and talk to your Gotami of all these stories, but remind him that if he bothers me any more, the white man's laws will be harsh on him . . . The people went away, their eyes full of disbelief because of the courage of the man. They knew that one day the spirits will confront the man, showing him their dark anger. They felt it was coming, but they simply said a man who refused to be warned only remembers the warning when his forehead is covered with wounds.

– Speak so that no one speaks for you. You have a mouth. Speak. Say what is in your heart, the ancestors pleaded with the man.

– My elders, it is not good punishment to cut off the mischievous hand of a child, the stubborn one said, his voice full of fear. He wanted them to forgive him, to send him back to his children so that he could teach them the ways of the land properly.

– You are not a child, an elder shouted at him. You are not a child. Can you not see the beard on your face? That is not a child's beard, warned the old man.

– In front of you, I am a child. I cannot do anything which you would not allow me to do, he went on. All the time he sweated, cursing at his unending desire for honey. It was honey which had sent him to this land of the honey of words. If he should go back to his people, he thought, he would never taste a drop of honey. He would find a medicine-man to cure his desire for honey.

– We forbade you from doing only a few things. We allowed you to plough the land, to drown the soul of the land with the white man's poisons, to kill the animals of the land with the poisons which the white man gave you. Those are bad things, but we said, the children are in trouble. They cannot be treated like a cigarette which burns at one end and is bitten the other end. So we allowed you to poison the graves of our fathers with the white man's medicines of the soil. The things that we said you should not do are not many. Yet you hardened the back of your head, thinking that the words of the dead are nothing. Now, we want you to harden your head so that we can talk. Talk is the medicine for troubles, the old men talked, their heads upright, their hands still as dead. The voices of the elders echoed in the distance, as if there were hills everywhere.

At his home, the man's people searched everywhere for him. He could not be found. Many stories are still told of how some people meet the man in his farm, roaming the fields at night like a secretary bird. Maybe he will roam the forest till the last days when all the people of the earth will come together from their wanderings, Johana told the boy.

Johana would teach Marko many other things so that the boy could respect the land of Gotami's people. She would show him how to fetch water from the farm well, how to pluck fruits from the wild trees. The boy listened like one mesmerized by a vivid dream. He would say yes all the time until Johana felt pity for him. He was such fertile soil even for the many lies which people told about the neighbour whom they said slept with his daughters before allowing them to be married. He was such fertile ground for anybody who did not respect the truth, she thought to herself.

Then after many years of his silence, Marko saw the anguished heart feeling it inside her. He had seen the wounds hatching deep inside Johana's chest. She had no words for him, such a young boy.

Marko saw the sisters of the boy of the tractor leaving her alone as they married the many young men who selected them. They left her without a word of good wishes. He also saw the silence which hung between her love for the man and his love for her.

Sometimes the man passed through on his way to play with his age-mates who sang and danced with the girls at soccer matches which they played on grass-covered pitches. Her man left her behind, creating many stories for her ears. She believed them but with a painful heart. She clung to the hope that one day he would change the thorny path he had chosen to walk. If a man walked along the path which had pits ahead, does he not come back and change his path? She knew what they said about the goodness of milk which does not need to be increased with salt. He would come back when the world said go back, to him. She lay there on the mat of her many nights and dreamt. The boy saw it.

Only the soil knows what is ailing the little child of a mouse, she heard the stories begin on lips which did not care too much for her. Johana heard them in her silence. What words would she say when she waited for what she hoped would come? She waited in the manner of a pregnant woman, in silence. It was better to wait in silence, she said to herself. Fortune falls on those who are quiet and silent, she recalled the words of the old women when they gave peanuts to those children who kept silent even when their bellies ached with hunger.

– I can see you are troubled, Marko told her one day. She

looked at him and nodded. He was young but with a sharp eye which could not be dismissed. He had learnt to see many things beyond her face which always carried laughter wherever she went.

– Everyone has their troubles, she said to him, trying to assure him that his was not an extraordinary discovery, but the boy continued to stare at her, his eyes pleading in a deep, silent way.

– Why should you suffer so much because of him? he insisted, already determined to take the place of the boy with the civet cat mouth. I am here, now grown up. She looked at him once more, begging him not to wound her on top of the injury she had received already. Many days and nights had passed, each bringing new pains to her wounds. Now he stood there, younger than her, a child warm from its mother's back, wanting to peep into the door of her love. How does she tell such a story to the people who cared about her?

Her father would kill her if his ears discovered that a mere herdboy had courage enough to stand in front of her, telling her with a straight face that he loved her. What had you shown the boy to give him the courage to say those words? she heard her father ask far away, his voice echoed by many elders in faraway lands which were only shadows in her memory. She had left those lands when she was a little girl. Now her memory only remembered the ways of the new place which was also strange in its newness. It is the noisy bird which gets the stone from the catapult, they would say to her.

She was afraid of herself, of the boy whose voice boomed in front of her like thunder. She was afraid of the land of Gotami's people. Strange things were not to be done in this land, she remembered. She feared too many voices of the land, voices of these people who did not know the burdens embedded deep in her heart. They saw her smile every day and said she was happy. How could they forget that the tooth is a witch, it smiles even at the murderer of one's mother.

For many many days to come, she did not see the falling fruit under the wild fruit trees. The river bathe in the flowing water annoyed her. Her skin refused to be touched by the gentleness of the cool water and the prickling sands of the river. Even the dust kicked up by the cattle returning home made her feel lonely. She was alone in her pain as the sun set and night swallowed her with her pains.

The day it happened, she had cast away all her fears and worries. She bathed down the river, not afraid of the crocodiles any more. Marko went to bathe behind the big rock, the one they said looked like the back of an elephant. This was the way it should be. Men must bathe alone, women must bathe alone. Then the boy came quietly to where she was in her nakedness. He saw the naked body of the woman, the unyielding body which she was willing to yield only to one man. He saw it splashed with fresh water from the river, glowing with a flame which only his eyes could see. The hand of the woman searched for the corners of the body where sweat could hide. He heard the woman sing about how the man rejected her, about how he causes her so much restlessness of the heart. She hummed the tune he knew so well, a song about rejection, neglect . . .

You cast me away
Like the skin of a snake,
You cast me away
Like a shadow at sunset.
Look now,
My heart is restless,
Look now,
My heart is restless . . .

When the woman saw Marko, she did not move or speak. Only her eyes asked him to come and bathe with her. They exploded with the joy of such a thing ever happening to her who had become a reject. He obeyed her silent command, crept nearer her and lay on the sand, powerless, a victim, his blood doing many things to him, his heart lost in the dark caves of what he would never understand.

Later, she was to hold his hand, leading his cracked finger to touch what he had done to her. Her hand led his hand to her sex, to the very fireplace from which he himself had been forged. He felt it, blood oozing out of her. He felt a cold pain of shame flow through his body. She looked at him, her eyes shy, her chest protruding with fresh erect breasts which were the gourds from which a child would suckle fresh milk to its satisfaction. The boy stared in disbelief, stunned by her own courage to yield to him, his own courage to receive the love that he had yearned for without knowing it.

Then Marko too took her hand, leading her fingers to himself, to touch the pain she had caused him. Her eyes glowed. His eyes glowed and both of them knew what they had not known for many years, what they would not know again for many years to come.

For many days, she walked clumsily, her gait gone.

At home, those with itchy tongues whispered that someone had broken a waterpot before reaching the destination. The little girls in the playground sang about the girl who broke the waterpot when she had almost arrived. They sang about the girl with flabby breasts. She heard them in her sleep. She saw their lips singing it in their silence as they went about their daily work. She was there. She was not there. She was alone, with Marko in her dreams which she knew would be shattered by unkind hands, the same hands which pushed the waterpot from her head where it had sat so safely.

Johana's father had gone to sleep, contented with himself, his mind settled in the hazy comfort of the life that he won himself. His two sons had died, not of the wishes of their ancestors, but of the wishes of those who carried guns on their shoulders, those who said death must come to them too, but with a fight. The two sons' voices sometimes came to him, one hoarse and fatherly, the other boyish and pleading in its echoes. They came to him troubling his mind all the time, forcing him to leave the fields where he worked. He would go and sit in the shade of the big *musuma* tree at the centre of the fields.

Alone there, he saw the many streams of blood which flowed out of his children. The blood spurted out of the young bodies, everyone silent, afraid of death. He saw the silent tears which welled in the hearts of those who watched, silent tears which would not come out until many years later when it was safe to cry. They died like beasts, like wild animals deprived even of a good death, he said to himself. They cried and begged to be forgiven, but no ears listened to them. I knew one day something like that would happen. I knew it. When blood starts flowing, it will have no end, he mourned. Tears welled up in his eyes. He did not wipe them away. There were no tears to wipe away. It was the pain which wiped away the tears. The scars went too deep, he felt.

Johana's mother saw him in his deep solitude. She watched him and said he would be left alone. Why should a man not sit and look at the scars on his body, she said, restraining the younger wives who wanted to hold him in their hands, consoling him, kneeling before him, saying his praises so that he could gather the courage of his ancestors. He needs it, they said. He must not be allowed to die away like that. He needs the courage of his own people, they said.

But the older woman said that was not to be so. She told them how he woke up at night and talked with his ancestors. She told them how he argued with the ancestors every night, reminding them how they had abandoned the children, two children who had died like sheep, with cut throats and no proper graves. Johana's mother did not want the younger women to make him feel more pain than he already felt. If you feel pity for him, he will feel sorry for himself. That is pain too, she said. An injured man must not feel pity for himself, otherwise he will live in sorrow for the rest of his life. Thus, she had come to restrain them with words so that the man could learn to face his new scars with strength.

Somebody had broken the old mirror in which Johana's father had learnt to see himself. He stood there, alone, living, fighting to continue leaving, bleeding, but not wanting to yield to the final defeat. Yes, he would bleed, but who said all bleeding must lead to death? He would cry, but who said all crying is mourning? Do those overwhelmed with pleasure and joy not cry? That surely was not death.

Inside her heart, Johana's mother too did not understand the life which Johana's father had faced since the time Marko and Johana died of their own choice. That was many years ago, when the war against the white man was rumours from the mouths of drunks and strangers. How could it be that a man can be so deserted by everything? Even as he left the land of his ancestors in search of land for his children, did he not perform the ceremony in which all the rituals were done for the ancestors? He had told them that since they had taught him that buttocks cannot bring anything new, he was searching for what the itching foot can give. He was like the new migratory bird which did not abandon its home forever. The bird only went away so that it could come back happier, Johana's father had said to his ancestors. We do not leave so that we insult you, he pleaded. We leave so that your children can live long enough to be able to offer you sacrifices, he said. He pleaded with them not to be reckless. Not to close their eyes and fool themselves into thinking that everything so disappears. When a child breaks the laws of his ancestors he is punished, not killed, he said.

Johana's mother remembered how she knelt down with him, praising and pleading with the ancestors of their two families.

She remembered how she took the small gourd of beer, pouring it on the threshold of her hut for the ancestors. They had sprinkled some fine tobacco there too. She heard the words they spoke to the ancestors, pausing as if the ancestors would answer them instantly. She heard them and was happy that they would leave the land of their ancestors happy, satisfied in their hearts that the ancestors would not feel abandoned.

But as many things happened to her children, to her husband, to everyone, she wondered in her heart how such pain could flood one heart. Maybe no one knows Johana's father, she said to herself as she stooped deeper into that moment of endless pain. Maybe no one even knows him, she said, her eyes swollen with tears, her heart torn with wild doubts which she did not know how to keep in her small body worn out by years of suffering.

– We came here to change our life, she said to herself, aloud, but this life has changed us. Nobody can know that we are the same people who came here, she whispered, her heart heavy with death. She had seen death. She had lived with death. She did not find death a partner to take along a journey, even a short journey which would not last for long.

Many people saw how war had changed Johana's father. He is no longer the same Johana's father we know, they said. They saw him wake from his mat, silent, despairing. They saw how he no longer walked his fields with the same pride he had walked before. Many years ago, he walked the fields, touching his lush crops, smelling the flowers of the cotton plants as they bloomed. He would walk, seeing the dead insects which the white man's poisons had killed. Poor creatures, he said, why don't they look for some other flowers to drink from? He saw Johana herself, with the spray pump on her back, like a hunchback, spraying the plants so that the cotton reached good grades which gave money. He saw her and heard her sing strange songs of girls from these parts. It was not her fault. She knew no other songs to sing.

Johana was different, and he knew it had to be so. Which other songs did she know so that she could sing them for him, for herself, for the birds in the trees? It was good that she sang these strange songs of these parts. She had to learn to be in these parts.

Now he walked in the fields, afraid of himself, afraid of memories. These were the same fields his two sons had worked, dreaming with him of how life would change, how they would be another people, another family beyond the recognition of those who had seen them arrive poor and ragged. They had come to Gotami's land to change their lives, to fight those who had wanted them to become beggars. He walked and feared those memories.

After trying for many days, he did not walk the fields again. He remained silent like the little bird he saw dead in the maize fields many years ago when Gotami's land was fresh with life. Maybe it had eaten the little poisoned insect from the cotton fields, he thought. He saw the bird, silent, dying slowly, not singing about its pain. That was the way to die, he said to himself, silent, not singing. The war to take the land from the white man had come and gone. But his mind failed to understand this new war which came to devour the children of the land, all of them.

– But Johana's father, you must go to the fields like you used to do. It is not good for a man to wake and then lie down as if illness is defeating him. Johana's mother shook his heart a little.

– What does it help? I have walked there, in the maize, in the cotton fields, I cannot talk to them any more, he lamented. He knew in his heart that the words of the maize plants, the songs of the cotton plants could not be heard any more. He was deaf to their music. They were blind to his now shadowy presence. He did not know any more how to talk to them, how to ask for anything from them. Before, he had asked them not to yield to the burning sun so that his children can thank him for giving them a future. He asked the crops to obey his voice so that he does not regret why he abandoned the faithful crops of his ancestors in favour of the new crops. But now the words of the plants were no longer the same. No words came out from them. His own mouth was mute. Even his heart refused to beat to the heartbeat of the crops.

He knew that he would die, rejected by this new land, rejected by the soil which he had poisoned with the medicines of the white man. He would die, alone like those children, his own children, the other children too, who had died alone in faraway places without their fathers nearby to close their eyes in the ways of the ancestors. He did not know when, but he smelled death all the time. His voice sounded like death, but he insisted that elders must not show death on their faces. What will children do? Elders must teach children to face death, to accept that death is only part of a new beginning. Only then did the pain of death vanish into the sky like smoke from a bushfire.

Many of his neighbours had seen war, with its guns and its blood flowing from all corners of the land. You never know where blood may come from, they said, hating the sight of strangers whom they had welcomed with pride from the beginning of their days. What would a home be if no one came to visit it? they said. He believed those words too, in his heart. But the many guns in the land had come in the hands of many youthful strangers. They said they were fighting for the land, the soil, so that our fathers can be buried where they wish to be buried. They spoke kind words about their fathers, then they spoke bitter words about the white man and his ways.

Greed, they said, was the thing which drove the white man to take the habit of giving other people crumbs while he himself ate the fat from the land, the young people said.

Farmers listened to the young people, not questioning them, not insulting them. They were happy and proud that their young children had seen it fit to challenge the white man to a big wrestling contest. Who is not proud when his son goes hunting for the first time, challenging the leopard and the lion, alone in the bush? they said. They felt a deep sense of pride in the young people who challenged the mysterious words of the white man which were spoken in strange tongues. The young people said the white man was a pauper in his own lands, that was why he had run away so that he could steal other people's lands. Have you ever seen a chief leaving his own lands to go and become something else in other lands? the young people spoke. The elders listened, their hearts glowing with joy at the words of truth which they heard from their own mouths, the mouths of their own children.

But sometimes they were torn with doubts. They doubted how it was possible that the white man can be defeated since he was the one who had made the guns which the children carried, slung on their shoulders. They wondered in their hearts whether these rugged children who grew up on pumpkin leaves and sadza would sit in the white man's office the way the white man did.

Johana's father too, doubted with them. He had seen how the white man held the pen in his hands, how he drank his tea without offering it to anyone who was in the office. That was the magic of the white man, he said to himself for many years, praying that the *Nkosi* be saved from losing his temper. He had heard stories of how destructive the temper of the white man was. A man who loses his temper and burns other people's granaries was to be feared, Johana's father thought.

Was the white man not the maker of guns? the farmers asked. Was he not the owner of these crops which give us so much money? they wondered. How was it possible that these young men promise so many things which the white man with his power had never promised them? The elders asked the children in their own homes, not those with guns. They warned their own children not to trust the words coming from a man's mouth. They saw in their own children a deep desire to join those who came with guns to fight for the soil. The heart of the children danced with so many dreams already flooding them.

– They say there will be jobs for all of us, said the young children in school. The parents saw how determined the children

90

were to join their fighting brothers. The man who refused the words of others only saw his folly in the scars of his forehead, the elders said.

Then many things happened. Many other people with guns came, telling them stories of war, how they would fight to the bitter end, destroying the terrorists from the forests.

– We came back from the bush, they said, because now people of our own blood rule this land.

Johana's father was confused. Many of those he thought gave wise words were also confused. They did not know what to do. The children went in many ways, joining whoever came to ask them to join, carrying guns to fight for many more things than what the first fighters said they would fight for. That was when Johana's father left his own home, abandoning his children who had refused to join any of the groups which carried guns. Many people would warn them to run away to relatives, somewhere, but the children said they had not insulted anyone who carried guns. Why should they run away? Where would they run away? they asked, puzzled. They had no relatives in the city where others went to hide. Their only refuge were the grass huts which sheltered them from the rain and the wind. This new rain of guns, they did not know how to shield themselves from it.

So they were insulted with many names. They did not know which ones fitted them. Some called them the ones who did not know that times had changed. Others called them sell-outs.

Even on the day Johana's two brothers were killed, they did not know what they were. They had refused to accept what people thought they were. So they died. Everyone knew they would die a bad death. They too knew it, but they waited, bitter in their hearts, but hopeful that death would spare them so that they could one day tell their children these tales. Fathers must live to tell their children these tales, they heard themselves say, their hearts heavy with blood.

All these things passed through Johana's father's mind as he lived the voices of his children. They were now mere voices, creeping through the inner ears, mauling at the ears inside him so that he heard them even if he did not want to continue hearing them. They were not loud voices. They were silent but loud, heard only by him and Johana's mother. That was the way of death, he said. Death mattered, not this life of crops and rains. He had lived the other life, but he still had to live the life of death. In a short time, death had taught him the many things which the life of rains and crops had not taught him.

It was like the eagle, he said, when the eagle flies, it is graceful and proud. It will only know the joy of flying in the sky the day it breaks its wings, he thought to himself. So many new things had confused him, dazzling his mind like a nightmare.

The day before they came for Johana's father I, his *vahosi*, saw many things on his face, wandering thoughts had come to him again. My mother told me when I was a girl, when the husband is not well, he sleeps with the *vahosi*, the first wife. I saw that Johana's father did not want to eat or drink anything. I touched his forehead with my palm. It was cold. How can the body of a grown up be so cold? How can it be so full of death? He even refused to wash his body, shouting at me for saying he was dirty. He was alone, like a traveller lost on the way, in the forests.

I went away into the forest, to fetch him some herbs which my mother told me long ago can help. I walked alone, thinking: Johana's father, what is this again which has entered you? Have I not seen enough of death in this strange land of Gotami's people? What has so annoyed the people of Gotami that they can allow all these things to visit me? I know that I gave birth so that I can live with death, but Johana's father is not my blood. He has his own people who know how to scold his ancestors if they think they are not protected well. But me, what have I done that

I enter this playground invaded with death? I am only a woman who must be married. Is that a crime?

I spoke with the trees, the hills, the caves. No one could hear me.

– Johana's father, try these herbs, I forced him to take some medicine.

– Johana's mother, there are some diseases which cannot be cured with herbs, he looked me straight in the eyes, like in those days when he looked at me and my heart danced the dance of many girls. Only that this time his eyes did not glow. The flame of his eyes was dead. They were dark and frightening.

– But Johana's father, hard things must be tried. Do they not say an old woman from Chivi once boiled stones, threw a pinch of salt in the pot before tasting them? That was in the year of the endless drought. Take these herbs, you never know, I said to him.

But I am only a wife. The day he married me, his people told me that I was like the one who had been given a gun to carry. Why should I be found to have fired the gun? To be asked to carry a gun is not the same as being asked to fire it, they told me with their own mouths.

That is the way they said our people see marriage. My people also told him the same words, that he had been given only the legs, the head belonged to its owners. If anything serious happened to me, he was to go to them, to say to them, there are things which I don't understand. That was the way it should be. I am only his wife. His people will help me, I said to myself. Everybody agreed with me.

Things were hard too, but who said that people must fold their arms when they are overcome by burdens? I saw them looking away all the time when I went to say to them, the problems of this family are no longer empty-handed, they mean more than what we see. They looked away from my face. How do you face a man on whose face you can see death? Death is not a thing to look at.

I will wait for them to give him a second burial. It may take long, but it is good to wait so that they will not say we told you so. Many days have passed now, the wind throwing more sand in my eyes, my heart sagging. Maybe the whirlwind will also take me one day. There will be so many second burials that no neighbour will come.

Some women marry husbands, others marry shadows of their dreams. They tell me I married death. My two sons died. My husband died. They did not fall ill all of them. Johana too, she cried. She dies every day too, somewhere in this land of Gotami's people. It is not many years since they all died, my husband, my sons, Johana, the one whose name people are now ashamed to give me.

It seems Johana had the key of death in the homestead. When she opened the house of death, death flooded out . . .

Marko looks at her, his eyes painful, his face heavy with many other burdens which he knows have thrown her life away like an old tortoise shell. He also knows that from now on life would be different. This was her body which had overwhelmed him. His body also, it had overwhelmed him, draining all the power in him. And on the sand, Marko sees patterns of stories of their life as if he were looking at a diviner's scattered bones. He knows Johana is now afraid of him. He has broken the shell of her shame, and she fears it. I think I will go away from here, he says to her. I will go back to my own people so that things can be as they were before, he speaks to her, as if to himself. She does not answer him or look at him. Johana looks only at herself, into herself to see the new life she has given away, to him . . .

Now so many deaths, no graves to look after near the anthills. Nothing. We fold our arms as if there is nothing to do. What can we touch? Everything we touch feels like death.

The night he was going to die was the worst. His stomach rumbled like the stomach of an elephant. He lay there, sleep refusing to visit his eyes, his breath fading, the heart caught in a whirlwind, pounding, kicking, jumping. Then I touched him on the chest, so that my fingers could know where the pain came from. He lay there and pretended not to feel my pained hands on his chest. I felt sweat all over his body, flooding the hairs of his chest like one walking in the rain.

When the door was opened in the dark night, I do not know where he found the strength to spring up from that sleep of death. He looked at those intruders, the people whose faces were like shadows. He looked at them, tears welling in his eyes. It was dark, but I heard the tears in his voice.

Then I knew they would take him far away from me, from this land which he had taken so many years to work on, the soil for which he had suffered for many years. They have come to kill the source, my heart told me. Yes, they had come to kill the source. Johana was dead, my two sons were dead too. Now they came to fetch the source of the river, the one from which all the water of the river comes.

This is his land, I said to myself, crying, mourning him already as they took him away, barefoot, to die in the forest like a rogue. They allowed him to wear his big coat, the one which those old soldiers brought from Hikira's wars. He wore it and they took him away, dragging him like a rag, a thief caught with his hand on the goat he was stealing.

I saw them take him away, being swallowed by the darkness, going to meet his death. As he stepped out of the house I felt the tears of my heart roll down my cheeks, rolling down, creeping away into my mouth, making me taste the bitter salt of the many years I lived with him. The tears rested on my breasts, making them sticky with the wetness, telling me that this was the end of the long journey we walked together. Every journey ends in sweat, the tears said to me. But I knew that every journey ends in blood, so much blood, the blood whose source I knew well, the blood I feared like the whirlwind.

The way of birth is the same, but the way to die, so many ways, all of us. But they took him away, to kill him like a goat that is slaughtered for the visitors. They did not say who they were, but they said they wanted to kill all sell-outs. They said he

95

had sold them out to those who fought them, those who did not want their enemies to know where they got food since they also wanted the wild fighters to die of hunger in the forest. They are bandits, dissidents, the radio always said, about the new ones who came to fight in anger.

If a man with a knobkerrie came to my home to ask for food, what can I do? Can a woman like me wrestle with a man with a gun, wanting to eat? You do not have to force me to give you food, strangers are given food every time they come to a home. Why would they force us?

But they came, with guns on their shoulders, telling us all the time that someone had wronged them. How can we be treated like women when we are in the bush together fighting wars? We cannot have leftovers when others are eating the fat of the land, they said to us.

I saw them saying it. I heard it with my own ears. They were angry children, saying all the things we had heard before. It was the same words. They said the enemy had changed his colour, that was all.

Many months after Johana's father returned from where he had hidden, Johana's mother tells him how everyone had become a stranger to Johana's father. Our life here has been difficult, Johana's father. No one says he knows you. They say it is dangerous to know Johana's father. It is death. So no one knows Johana's father. When they say things about you, they first look for a place to hide so that no ears can steal their words. Every time they pass your ruined houses, they simply look and shake their heads in silence. In their hearts I know they pity you, the man who brought up a family so that death can have a feast. Oh, how the ancestors are merciless! How God is merciless. He let the man travel from Gutu, in faraway places, to bring him here so that he can die so far from the land of his ancestors. How his grave should have been there so that his wives can see it, so that they can swear by the dead lying in the anthill. But they will not say all those things with their mouths. They will say them with their hearts and shake their heads as if Johana's father is the first person to die.

When the story-tellers gather around the fire, they will one day tell the story of a man who ran away from death. Every time he heard about death, the man ran away. So he decided that one day he would go away, to lands so far away that death would get lost searching for him. The man packed all his belongings, his children, his wives, his clothes, everything. He got them together, even the dogs and the cats which he liked so much but hated the idea that they would die one day. He took them along with him.

When the man arrived in the strange lands far away, he met an old man, drunk but on his feet. He put his belongings down and went to talk to the old man. Is this the land without death? he asked. The old man looked at him and laughed. You are dead already if you are in this land, the man sang, staggering away towards what looked like endless mountains of darkness.

The man decided to build a house for himself and his family. He would sit there day and night, singing about this land of death. His ancestors came to see him one day. They told him that his singing made the land of death a better place than where he had come from. So he should stay there, with death around him and wait to join them.

That is what the story-tellers will tell the children around the fire for many years to come. Death, the sharp knife that cut so many trees and smiled at its own work. Death, the axe that cut all the trees of the land, leaving only barren land so that we the living can shed tears as we look at the barrenness. Death, why did you leave me alone, no children, no husband, no friends.

There are names which are dangerous to know. Johana's father is a bad name to know. I knew him when we were young, our eyes stealing into each other, into our hearts. But when I met him I did not know that this was the name of death. Death only came when I had emptied my womb of all that I could give him,

97

three children. Death ran after them all, overtook them, and grabbed the father, the source of the blood which watered Gotami's land.

I am waiting here, under this *musuma* tree, not for the fruits that fall, but for the blood, the death that comes to me too. I will not pick the fruits even as they ripen above my head. I will not pick them. I will sit here, waiting for death to come whichever way it wants to come.

Death, come and sit here with me. Come and be my friend, my shadow which only sleeps when the sun goes away for more fire. I will not invite death the way Johana invited death to a feast. I will wait for this death which is with me always so that people will say: the house of death is the house of death, look at what is happening to the house of death. I will not allow the mouths of people to say those words. Those are unkind words which invite death. I know mine is the house of death, but I wait, like a young woman waiting for her lover to come back from his first hunting trip.

For many years, Johana's father's neighbours did not know what to say about this house of death. They were born with death in their hands, they said. How can death come so many times to one house? They saw themselves looking at death all the time they passed near Johana's father's home. Some said they had eaten the fruit of death, the one which made the eater smell of death so that when death came to look for its victims, it smelled them out and took them away. But this kind of death, they said. This kind of death is something else. People must die well.

The whole of Gotami's land had not seen any such death before. They had not seen a family invaded by death so much. What kind of death is this which does not know how to rest? What kind of death is this which has no shame? they wondered.

The men with guns had come one day, to a farm, little children playing outside. They were silent, sitting there on the logs near the cattle pens, young men with faces darkened by too much stay in the forest where they did not sleep properly. It was only later that they called the men and women on the farm.

– We have to tell you that we are here, they said. Those of you who do not know that the enemy has changed the colour of his skin would have to know soon, they told the farmers. They said they were men who were treated badly after the war to free the land from the hands of the colonizers. It was they who had fought the white man from the west, defeating the enemy until he said talk was better than fight. The talking did not give the owners of the land what they had been fighting for since the coming of the white man. They said they told the people who had talked for them that they must not accept crumbs from the people who had robbed them of their land. No, if you are given crumbs, do not accept them. Say those who sent us are prepared to fight until the end of the earth, the young people said.

The radio said those young men were bandits who wanted to drink the blood of the defenseless people of the land. Every night the voices from the radio insulted the young men in the bush, they were infidels, murderers who killed everyone they came across, the voices shouted.

Even the voices of the big people who had taken over the rule of the land, they insulted the young men every day. It is said they had quarrelled with them about many things. So the young men went away into the bush to find the guns they had hidden when they were freedom fighters in the bush. They took the guns and remained in the bush, killing anyone whom they thought was eating from the same pot with the new rulers.

It was painful, the farmers said. It was painful to have war for so many years. The heart must rest. Fear is not a good thing to remain in the hearts of the people for so long, the farmers said to themselves. Why do they not talk with those who are now ruling? Were they not the same people who carried guns and said they would set every piece of land free from the rule of the white man? Were they not the ones who fought the war from the west so that

99

the enemy was like one stung by many bees at the same time? Now that the white man had said take your land, why do they not sit down in the way of the ancestors and talk these things over? The medicine for burdens of the heart is talk, the farmers said.

They talked among themselves, only to those they trusted. The tongue can also be the kindler of a big fire, they thought. It was better to keep silent. A quiet man is safe from the insults of those who think a fight is like food which you eat every day. It was better to close the mouth so that when an angry man talks his bad words to you, he will feel shame in his heart, they said and sealed their mouths.

The young men went round, even during the day, asking for the people to cook for them as it was before the white man was defeated. They began to sleep in houses, expelling the owners of the houses. They too did not want to suffer the bite of the many mosquitoes which sang hymns at night, searching for the blood of the farmers. Sometimes they took the women to dark places, making them pregnant.

Then the old men and women were sad with the new rulers. They could not understand how it was that people who had fought the same enemy could become greedy when the enemy ran away. They must learn that chieftaincy is taken in turns, others whispered. Others asked what chieftaincy is if it is not shared. What is a chief without good followers? they asked in the silence of their sleep, waiting for death, waiting for sunrise when they could see the wielders of guns from far away so that they could run to the forest where they would hide until the wielders of guns went away too, to other lands, with their guns.

We do not like guns, they talked inside their hearts. Guns are not food, they continued, afraid all the time that there were so many things which they did not understand any more. There was no one to talk to. The new rulers, their own children, also talked the white man's tongue. How could they go to them, in their ignorance of the white man's ways, and say to them, talk with your brothers so that we do not have guns instead of food. We want our children to go to school singing the new songs of our freedom. Talk so that you can hear each other's words and clear the path of misunderstanding which you are now walking.

They wanted the big people to talk, to sit down with gentle words in their mouths, not guns. No one eats guns, they said. These guns must be locked away so that people can talk properly. The pain inside them told them it was the pain which said so many things which they had not thought of before. It said to them, the land was now theirs, but they could not farm it. Guns stared at them all the time. Their cattle roamed like wild animals. They would be stolen by anyone who braved the land infested by guns. The pain told them that the white man was happier than before, on the lands which he had stolen from their ancestors. Were there no songs which they had inherited, songs to say to the white man, we have come to take away land which your fathers took from our fathers? What was it, their pain told them from the heart, that the white man had eaten, that he should be left alone to eat the fat from the land when the owners of the land starved? What was it that made the white man, who had been threatened with death, be awarded as if he had not stolen the lands through war? They overwhelmed themselves with many questions which dizzied their minds, people used to farming their lands, watching the sky all the time, wondering when the raindrops would come to save them from the mouth of hunger.

The roads in Gotami's land grew thick forests. No one came to cut down the trees. The farmers heard how road workers had been killed whenever they attempted to make the roads. No one wanted to work in the lands of guns. They wanted to enjoy the fruits of the new freedom which they had never tasted before in the rule of the white man. The farmers were left alone, only listening to the insults of the big people over the radio. They shout bitter words from afar, the farmers said. This is not time for harsh words. It is time for gentle words so that the young people with guns can agree to sit down and say what had provoked them.

But the big people far away did not listen. They wielded guns to shoot all the young men in the bush. They told everyone they would finish them if they were not given food by the villagers and the farmers. They would finish them, with guns.

People are blind, Johana. The stump that hits the toes of the person walking in front of you will also hit the toe of the person walking behind. When the big finger burns, the small ones also burn. That is the way to see the life of people.

Johana held a bottle in her hands, her fingers itching with the desire to hold it for the last time. These were the fingers which held the blood of love on Marko's body. Now they held the blood of death. She looked at the bottle, hid it in her apron pocket and walked stubbornly into the sooty hut, the one in which they cooked the family food. She walked alone, feeling that this was the time to be alone. She did not want any eyes on her. Even the little darkness which already engulfed her annoyed her. She walked alone, her feet sometimes trembling, sometimes steady, not wanting to collapse and give her away to those who would ask what it was that made her fall.

The fall of mountains makes so much noise, she heard herself say, but the fall of ants does not. She was the ant which would fall, quietly, without a noise. Her mind was made up. The boy who sang on the tractor had left her alone, without a word. Her father, Johana's father, had left her alone. Soon, her own mother would leave her alone. Maybe she was tired of being left alone. Maybe she feared the loneliness of one left alone by so many people, those who should have clutched her to their chests. She was alone and feared it.

In the cooking hut, she put out the fire. No eyes should see her. She hated eyes. The blind were happy, she said. They did not have to see the land in which people just walked away from you when they should hold your hand. They did not walk alone, her inner voice said.

But now she wanted to walk alone. She wanted to take the first and last step, to give the last footstep to her own piece of earth, chosen by her. That was the way it should be. Those who rule the land never go so far as to say on which piece of earth every footstep should go, she thought. I have chosen my own piece of earth where my last footprints should be.

Johana was not like the insect which she sprayed with poison in the cotton fields every rainy season. She was different. The insects had come to the cotton flowers to feast, to drink the juice that overwhelmed them with its sweetness. It was a sweetness which was irresistible. She was not like that. She had seen how the sweetness of the flowers caused the death of the little creatures. They lay there on the soggy earth, stretching their legs with death, with a pain whose words she did not know. They lay there, rugged, formless, writhing with the many drops of pain inside them.

She had felt the pain of the insects inside her body, but ignored it. There was some pain which did not matter. Was it not so also with many other pains which she had ignored? The tiny thorn pricks from the grass thorns. She ignored them. Or the pain from the fight of a small calf as it tried to chase her away from the udder of the cows she milked every day. Such pain must be ignored, she felt. So she had learnt to ignore the pain of the insects, or the little birds which died after eating the dead insects. She saw them die and thought they had chosen to join the small dance of death.

But what was this dance she was now about to join? Who would dance it with her? Would she dance it alone just as she

103

had walked alone for so long? Who would be brave enough to take the bold step into the fire? Fire burns. She did not know who would offer themselves to join a walk through the fire. But for herself, her mind was made, her dreams completed.

She looked at the sooty walls, and the thatch grass of many years, black like the coming night. She was happy there was no moonlight outside. Moonlit nights are not the nights to leave the arena for such a long sleep. That cannot be. They are nights for the dance of boys and girls, those who sing so loud, welcoming the moon. She heard the moonlight boys sing to her with voices from far away into the memory of her life, her days when she stood there with them and felt they sang her songs too.

Moon, bring me leaves
Bring me a wife.
Moon, bring my bride
Bring me life.
Moon, bring me a firefly.
Bring me a fireplace.

She heard them sing from far away. She wanted to join them, a deep urge welling up in her. She heard them, their voices wafting in the wind, sometimes hitting her ears with the harshness of a slap, sometimes fading away, forcing her to strain her ears to hear what the boys were saying. She knew their words, but she wanted to hear them again, to allow them to settle on her heart like fresh morning dew.

Johana held the bottle of pain in her fingers, and the boys refused to sing to her. Their voices died. They did not sing to her as she danced this dance of death. They stared in their silence, their voices dead. She did not need their voices, the voices of little creatures which she saw die every day. She wanted to be alone, without song, without dance, without voices. She was silence itself, muteness.

The liquid inside was dull and thick, colourless. She had smelt it before as she carried the spray pump on her back like a hunchback. She did not know how it would taste on her supple tongue. She did not know how it tasted on the tiny tongues of the insects in the cotton field. She did not even want to know. The insects were not there to tell her. They had died many seasons ago, all of them. Some remained, the stubborn ones which fought death with their wings and long, thin mouths. Others died, the ones with a wild appetite which made them swallow what they had not cooked.

She opened the bottle of pain, glancing at the closed door as she did so. Then she put the bottle down and walked to the dirty wooden door, tied it to a metal hook with a wire and went back to confront her new dance partner. He was there, silent, mute. She would not speak to him again, this dancer who sat there like an abandoned child outside the dance arena in the moonlight.

When she lifted the bottle to her mouth for the third time, she did not hear the violent hands which tried to open the door of the hut. She was deaf to any new visitors who wanted to disturb her dance of death. She was too busy dying to hear her little sister's voice, shouting, cursing, the little feet kicking at the wooden door.

Deep into the night, they sang for her only the songs of death. She was not to hear them. She was not to hear her father's voice of death as it whirled above all others. She did not see her mother lumped on the dusty earth, other women holding her body, consoling her. Johana did not even hear the little voices of her little sisters who wondered what dance this was which was danced with tears on the face.

Johana was alone. She would be alone for many years to come. She did not want to know that even her father would not have the courage which she took. Others would take the courage for him so that he did not have to weigh his heart down with the pain of deciding to die.

She died knowing that Marko's body lay drowned, deep in the new water well which her father's hands had dug. But she died not knowing that Marko's body would be found hanging from a *munhondo* tree only a few paces from the roof of the sooty hut where her hollow body lay, eaten away by the poison from the bottle.

They came to *famu namba* 145 pointing the wrong way, when Johana's father was sleeping. He shared the warmth of his bed with his first wife, Johana's mother. Sometimes he felt he should change the way people called his first wife, also the way they called him. Johana had died many years ago. What was the use of keeping her name in their hearts? Sometimes he felt the name should die too. But he did not know what ritual to perform so the name might have been buried with the one who carried it in her heart.

Strong men came many years after Johana's mother had received her husband from Petronella's unkind hands. Nobody talked about those years, mad years of guns which fired so many bullets that the white man said let us sit down like men and talk about these things. After all, we are people all of us. The strong men said they were young men who ran away from the army. Some said the other people in the army had taken away their guns so that they could whip them like small boys. Others said the young men were used to carrying guns. They could not be persuaded to walk around like women, selling vegetables on the market place.

They banged the old door of the hut of Johana's father and broke in with anger and force. Without any words, they lit a small flame inside the hut. The small cracks in the fireplace showed where Johana's father had been lying. He was already up, standing against the wall of mud and wood.

– Who are you? he shouted with fear. What do you want? He saw dark faces half-lit by the dull light coming from the small torch in the hands of the intruders whose shadows he saw in the intense darkness.

– We are the people you sold-out, the voice from a dark figure said.

– We know all you have said about the soldiers. Your two sons died in the war because of you. You taught them to sell-out. You ran away to the city where you spent many years pretending to be mad. Now you are back. We are fighting a different kind of war. You start selling us out again. What sort of man are you? they went on with many bitter words which made Johana's mother weep for him as he stood there. Why had she spent sleepless nights looking for a good medicine-man to clear his head? Why had she spent many words assuring people that now things were better, troubles cannot come where other troubles are? Why had she told her god in her silent prayers at the church that even when she thought he had betrayed her, now she will die happy because Johana's father is back? Why? Why?

– I did not sell-out anybody. I don't know who you are, he took courage, his knees weak, his heart sagging, blood already flowing from his throat.

He saw his own blood in the darkness. He felt it creep like a little lizard, down the throat, on to his shoulders, down the trousers until it clogged on the big toe, in his shoe. He felt it. He was dying. They were cutting his throat slowly so that he could feel the pain. He heard himself breath the last breath, his nostrils blocked with clogged blood.

– Come with us. Make any noise and you are dead, the shadow said.

The walked for most of the night, in the dark, stopping to listen, changing direction, running at times, forcing him to drag on even when he thought he would fall headlong on to the stony ground hardened by the many years of drought. Up the hill, down the valley, into the dense forest where no one would see Johana's father for many days after they killed him.

They sat him down on a log. He slumped like a man carrying a burden many times heavier than his body. Sweat shimmered in tiny rivulets out of him. He did not wipe it away. Sometimes he licked at the sweat near his lips, to quench the thirst of so many hours of walking without rest.

– We want to kill you very nicely. I am sure you have never died like that before, the man laughed, his face showing faintly in the ominous darkness of a morning already being greeted by so many birds, so many little insects which played music with their wings and little mouths.

The owl was not hooting any more. The morning brought fear under its feathers. It was silent. Only the weaver birds sang their morning greetings to the sky as it slowly gleamed for the coming of the new day. New journeys began with the rising of the sun. Small birds flew as their hearts told them where the next ripe fruit was. Big birds circled up in the sky, searching the grains of sand beneath, looking for the lone squirrel which had not felt the fire from the eagle's claws.

After many days, Johana's father's body was found. Johana's mother said she only saw him when they took him away from her bed. She could not point with her fingers any direction, any path she thought they could have taken. Why would they go this way and not that way? she asked herself. She shrugged her shoulders when they asked her about the faces of the men, what did they look like? Their bodies, were they tall or short? Did they have thick voices or voices like women? Johana's mother did not want to speak. She remained mute, burning inside herself with pain, mountains of pain which she carried inside her alone.

It took them many days to find the body of Johana's father, stuffed in a hollow log. Dogs ate his lips and wound up the feast with gnawing at the bones inside the flesh. Jackals too came when the dogs were not there. They chuckled and mewed to frighten away their enemies.

Do not touch this body, said a note left at the scene of the death of Johana's father. Sell-outs should not be buried, went on the note. Signed DIZDENTS.

Johana's mother refused to go and see the body.

– Nobody knows Johana's father, she said, shrugging her shoulders in resignation.

At the farmers' association, the place where they told Johana's mother to go for help, they look at her in her torn dress. She stands there in tears, wondering what the young man in front of her thinks about her. She is ashamed to be so poorly dressed. She feels her presence insult the man in front of her.

– Maybe I can get some help to bring up the few remaining children, Johana's mother says, her words fading.

– What was the name of your husband? the man nibbles at the pen in his hands.

– Johana's father, she says, tears slowly trickling down her cheeks. She feels them flow down her face like a little ant walking on the face of a sleeping child. She does not wipe them away. She is weak, the tears are strong. She is weak, her eyes are weak too. She waits for the answer from the man. She waits for many years, looking at him, looking at herself, inside herself, outside at what life has done to her, so many scars, so many wounds, so many darknesses in her eyes. She wonders inside herself how it is that life gives light to others while it gives darkness, gloom, gloom to others.

She coughed, breathing her pain away.

– No one knows Johana's father, the man says.

No one knows Johana's father, the words echo in the caves of her heart, in the caves of her mind. She walks away, feeling as if Johana's father had been an insult all his life. But she had loved him, sharing the warmth of her bed with him, bearing children with him, some dying, others living when the ancestors allowed it.

No one knows Johana's father, the people sang, many years later when these stories could be told without any danger to the story-tellers. They sang and danced to the songs about this shadow which came with the sunrise and died at sunset, blown away by the wind, carried on the wings of the sun.

When Johana's father still walked the land, his smile always on his face, no one talked about him. But now, things had changed. His name was the name of death. No one wanted to die, so no one talked about him without calling his friends to some hidden place where there would be no ears stealing into their conversations.

Johana's father, he would have to wait for many more years to be buried properly in the way of the ancestors. He would wait until the vulture and the jackal which ate his body died so that they too could be buried. That would be the only way to bury him. The farmers could not bury him. They had nothing to bury. Those who now ruled the land said no one knows Johana's father. So they could could not even mention his name when those who died fighting wars were mentioned. His name was not there all the time.

It would be like that for many years to come, for many seasons of rains and droughts, seasons when birds sang and danced on top of the trees, praising the new rulers for the new rule of the land which their fathers had given them. It would be so, for many years, even to the mountains which stared at Johana's father's bones scattered in the caves, valleys and ravines. The trees too, would stare at the bones whose owner they did not know, and say, was his house the house of death?

No answers would come to them, but they knew there were questions to ask, many questions to which there would be no answers, words without ears to fall on, wasted words because no one knew Johana's father, and Johana's mother knew all these things as she waited for her own death also, sleeping on the same mat on which Johana's father slept before death visited this house of death.

*

Johana's mother hears the echoes of the new lullabies from the lips of the mothers carrying silent children. She hears them sing about the red moon is blood, the eye of the bull is a bullet, the girl's long neck is a needle. She hears it all in the silence of this house of death where life would have to start anew, like the dead leaves that would have to rise again from their death.